Sin Hellcat

LAWRENCE BLOCK
DONALD E. WESTLAKE
writing as Andrew Shaw

SIN HELLCAT

LAWRENCE BLOCK & DONALD E. WESTLAKE
writing as ANDREW SHAW

Cover and Interior Design by QA Productions

A LAWRENCE BLOCK PRODUCTION

Classic Erotica

---

21 Gay Street
Candy
Gigolo Johnny Wells
April North
Carla
A Strange Kind of Love
Campus Tramp
Community of Women
Born to be Bad
College for Sinners
Of Shame and Joy
A Woman Must Love
The Adulterers
Kept
The Twisted Ones
High School Sex Club
I Sell Love
69 Barrow Street
Four Lives at the Crossroads
Circle of Sinners
A Girl Called Honey
Sin Hellcat
So Willing

Classic Erotica #22

SIN HELLCAT

Lawrence Block
Donald E. Westlake

CHAPTER 1

I saw Jodi again the other day. She's a whore now making twelve thou a year, doing quite well at it. I remember, way back in college days, thinking to myself, now, Jodi's not the marrying type. There stands (or sits or lies prone) a career woman if there ever lived one. It was nice to know I'd been right, and that she was doing so well.

She offered me some, no charge of course, for old time's sake, but I just couldn't get into the mood. I mean, it would be like taking free legal advice. I mean, it's the girl's *profession*.

So we sat around at her place—lovely little apartment in a hotel on Lexington Avenue—and talked over old times together, college days and what happened to so-and-so, and what we've both been doing since, and we both got a little smashed on Scotch—a bottle of Vat 69 given her by one of her admirers for some symbolic reason or other.

It had been ten years since I'd seen Jodi, and Lord how she'd changed! Those huge soulful dark eyes were even deeper and more level and piercing than they'd been when she was twenty-one and could still remember back to the loss of her virginity. And her body had filled out very nicely—lovely surging breasts and firm hips and the kind of solid thighs that can constrict a man if he doesn't watch himself—the inevitable result, I suppose, all that filling out, of her constant activity. She'd had two more abortions since last we'd met, she told me, making a grand total of three, and the unlicensed fraud who committed (I can't say performed) the third one slipped a bit, and now dear Jodi can rest assured that there will never be opportunity or necessity for a fourth.

It was mid-afternoon, a Tuesday in fact, and so both early in the day and early in the week for Jodi to be down and about, making a living. She was wearing a green knit sheath dress—it went well with her naturally-tanned complexion and honey-blonde hair—and she persisted in crossing her legs, revealing the long tanned underslope of one rounded thigh. That was distracting as hell, but I averted my eyes, and compromised by looking intently at her breasts instead, outlined individually by the tight green knit, proclaiming twice that she wore no bra beneath.

I knew I'd get a grumbly sort of hell from Marty for not coming back to the office after lunch, but this old school reunion was just too good to miss. Besides, I had all my copy in on the Dexter Frozen Dinners—"A Square Deal On A Square Meal"—and didn't really have anything to do until I got the go-ahead from the Dexter people. So old time-clock Marty could go to hell with himself. I would spend a quiet afternoon here with dear old Jodi, and take my normal train back to Helen.

I thought of Helen, my wifey-wife, the frigid witch of the Ramopos, icily waiting off in our Rockland County suburban hide-a-wee, and I glanced again up under Jodi's green skirt, and I shuddered at the contrast.

We sat and chatted and got quietly snockered, and I contemplated sliding the palm of my hand up along that thigh, fingers extended, and in a happy glow composed of one part Vat 69 to one part reminiscence, I remembered the first time I had ever taken dear old Jodi to bed . . .

Spring of my sophomore year, it was, twelve years ago. I was nineteen, only recently devirginized myself, and suddenly discovering in me some of the common aspects of the bull, with the exception that I seemed to be eager all the time.

It was Friday afternoon, I remember, in late May, and a bunch of us had cut classes to go down to the lake and swim. There were about twelve of us, evenly divided into boys and girls—which is always the best way, I think, after all—and we'd begun as simply an amorphous pack, only gradually pairing off. I'd taken Jodi to a movie once upon a time, but aside from some sporadic breast-clutching in the darkened balcony of the theater, nothing much had happened. I looked at her that afternoon, and I knew at once that that was a mistake that had to be rectified, and the sooner the better.

God, she was lovely! Picture this, if you'll be so kind: A girl of eighteen, just tall enough so that the top of her head was even with my shoulder. Long slender legs, tanned an amber gold. Smooth tanned arms, cameo shoulders and neck, the softest downiest throat in all creation. A longish pixyish face shaped somewhat like an inverted triangle. No! What a ghastly picture, that isn't what I mean at all! Picture an elf, with the straight slanting jawline, the high cheekbones, and somehow *hungry* look. Add to this picture a flawless tanned complexion, two huge round dark eyes as deep as night, a straight not-too-narrow nose, and cupid-bow lips of a red that would put Titian to shame. That was her face, framed by honey-blonde hair cut rather short and brushed very straight, curling around the shells of the ears.

I purposely left the portion encased in the bathing suit till last. The bathing suit itself, of course, was black. Two straps curved over those lovely shoulders and shot down toward the breasts. Firm breasts, not yet very large, but exciting to touch for all that. And, below, the bathing suit hugged down across a perfectly flat belly. And now we turn her around, as though she were a work of art upon a pedestal, and we stare for a while at the back view.

The lovely breasts around front distracted us so that we didn't really notice her waist. Now, with the aft portion facing us, we can see that she has a hell of a good waist indeed, the sides sloping in from beneath the arms—that's just a hint of breast-curve we can see there, when she raises her arm that way, and isn't that the most beautiful sight in all the world?—and the sloping-in ends at a waist that is just the perfect degree of slenderness, without the malnutrition look that goes over so big in the clothing ads. And below the waist, the whole business starts to slope out again, curving this way and that, in the cutest rear you've ever seen. You just want to walk up behind her and pinch, and lean your chin on that soft shoulder and whisper into that soft ear, "Hiya, Jodi."

That was Jodi.

At any rate, we all cut classes and went off to the lake for an afternoon of swimming and fooling around. It was, as I said, late May, and too early for the lake to be filled with tourists and vacationers and cabin-owners, so we had the place pretty much to ourselves. We ran shouting into the chilly water at the public beach and immediately swam around to one of the better private beaches, where we knew the owners hadn't yet put in their annual arrival. One poor fool—old Jack Fleming, I think it was—tried to swim the whole way one-handed, holding a portable radio up in the air with the other arm, and of course the result was that he practically drowned himself and gave that radio a hell of a good soaking.

But they really made radios in those days. We opened the silly thing up and let it dry in the sun for two or three minutes, and then we slapped it back together and turned it on, and by God it played! It played mainly static, of course, but here and there you could detect a note of music in the garble, so we turned it up to top volume and then spent the afternoon screaming over it.

I went after Jodi right away. She'd spent a short while going steady with a guy named Andy Clark, but he wasn't there that afternoon, and the whole thing between them was finished with anyway, so she was unattached, and I made damn sure I was the first one to attach myself to her.

It was the usual routine that afternoon. We swam around a while, and then we splashed each other, and chased each other around in the shoulder-deep water, and I dunked her a couple of times, and then I kissed her. Her lips were cool from the water, the rounded double-front of her bathing-suit-covered breasts was rough and exciting against my chest, and her waist, way down beneath the water's surface, was cool, the perfect size for my arm.

And she responded beautifully. She clung to me, her arms around my back, returning the kiss—eyes closed, in the manner of young girls everywhere—and when I parted my lips and probed hesitantly with a quivering tongue, she opened her mouth at once to accept it.

That was all, for a while. We splashed and chased and occasionally kissed, and finally I got my courage up—I was only nineteen, after all—and hidden beneath the water I slid my arm around her side, beneath her arm, and clutched her tender breast.

There was a difference. Why was there a difference? Even now, I don't know. All I know is that there was that difference, and that the difference always holds true. In the balcony of the movie theater Jodi's breasts had been soft and pliant, in feeling they were whipped cream mountains topped by wrinkled cherries. To touch those cherries was to make dear Jodi moan and writhe in delight. Underwater, encased in a bathing suit rather than blouse and bra, the breasts were firm and strong, the cherries as hard as anything one would want, and the whole thing, if possible, even more exciting than before.

The second time my hand fondled those wonderful breasts as we kissed, my other hand encircled her and cupped a rounded buttock, and she closed her eyes and moved against me, the water cool and invigorating, the vibrant girl in my arms too exciting to be stood, and I confess a wild oat was lost in the depths of the sea.

It was a long and—now I look back on it—horribly frustrating afternoon. We stayed in the water awhile, and then we stretched out on a blanket onshore, a bit away from the others, ostensibly to get some sun, but actually to get some fondling done. I caressed that precious body, leaned down to kiss the breasts with lips that grew stronger and harsher until at last her moans of pleasure were muffled by a stifled scream of pain, and my hand roamed the front of her body, building courage, stroking the coarse front of that bathing suit, moving ever closer, until finally she sighed and gripped me tighter and kissed me so furiously I thought she would break my neck.

But farther than that we could not go. Her bathing suit, top and bottom, was too snug-fitting. And there were, after all, ten other youngsters right nearby.

And so the afternoon was played away, with mutual frustration. Around seven, one of the more organizational-minded males of our group took up a collection for food and drink—I donated two dollars, I remember—and went away, to shortly return with pizza and beer, the pizzas cold and the beer warm. But we were all young, and hardships didn't bother us, so we ate the cold pizza and drank the warm beer, and at every opportunity I caressed Jodi's fantastic body.

It must have been around eight o'clock when one of our group mentioned the baseball game. Now, here's the situation: Every college worthy of the name has the three intercollegiate sports, football and basketball and baseball. And our college was, in that respect, worthy of the name. Now, everyone attends the football games, of course, particularly when one's own team is an odds-on favorite to win, which ours inevitably was, and about half the normal student body jumps at the chance to watch a basketball game. But no one in college goes to look at a collegiate baseball game, absolutely no one. Why this is I don't know, but it is. We twelve had, therefore, neither the knowledge that a baseball game was to be played by our jolly team tonight, nor much interest in what the hell our baseball team was doing *any* night.

And so it was that the announcement that our baseball team was playing an away game that very night was met, at first, with an overwhelming display of public apathy. At first. But then someone else—or it might have been the same person, I no longer remember—suggested that it might be a great oddball idea to go watch this here baseball game, cheer our team extravagantly, and get happily mashed.

The concept of going to a college baseball game was so radical, so unexpected, so completely absurd, that we all, naturally, agreed at once, and immediately began to pack the remaining beer into auto backseats, while two of the drivers huddled together over a roadmap, trying to find out (1) where the hell Ylicaw, where the game was to take place, might be, and (2) how the hell to get there.

Then someone came up with a disgusting thought. "Hey!" cried this someone. "What kind of baseball team do we have, anyway? Are they good or are they lousy?"

A quick headcount demonstrated that no one present knew what kind of baseball team we had.

"I don't want," said this someone, "to watch our lousy baseball team get beat."

True enough. But the problem was solved by someone else, who said, "Hell, we won't know which team is ours, anyway. What difference does it make?"

None at all, obviously. We piled into cars—Jodi curled beautifully upon my lap—and tore away in the general direction of Ylicaw.

We got lost, of course—several times—which didn't bother me in the least. I was scrunched into a corner of the back seat, Jodi on my lap, and my hands and lips were kept very busy indeed. By the time we finally did straggle into Ylicaw, I was as eager as a

Cape Canaveral launching pad and as frustrated as a soap opera heroine. You could have fried an egg on me.

Ylicaw, by the by, was the other side of a state line or two, so I suppose I should have spent the next twenty years in jail. My purposes, concerning Jodi, were about as basic as it is possible to get.

At any rate, what with leaving the lake so late and getting lost now and again, we arrived at the greenwood stadium in Ylicaw just in time to watch our school bus pull away, toting the ball team back home again. We had managed to miss the game.

So there we were in the thriving metropolis of Ylicaw at ten-thirty of a weekday evening. None of us had ever been in that town before—what possible reason would anyone have for going to Ylicaw?—and from the look of the place we had arrived too late to watch them roll up the sidewalks.

We clambered out of our two-car caravan and conferenced around a lonely streetlight. There were no other pedestrians in sight. The stadium—barely large enough to deserve the name— lay shrouded in darkness, a condition shared by all the buildings we could see up and down the street. The only bit of neon in sight belonged, believe it or not, to a feed store.

And so we talked it over. We had come all this way, with great difficulty, and none of us wanted to simply turn around again and drive all the way back. We had to *do* something first, doggone it!

Unfortunately, Ylicaw was about the most unlikely spot for *doing* something that any of us had ever seen. At least that portion of it in view was pretty unlikely.

We finally decided to split into scouting groups, each heading off in a different direction, and we would all reassemble here at the cars in half an hour. If there was any life to be found anywhere in Ylicaw, one of our scouting parties would find it.

Jodi and I were a complete scouting party. We started walking, turned two corners, walked an additional block, and discovered a park. It was a small and dark and empty little park, about the size of a desktop, sporting grass and trees and assorted shrubbery and a couple of footpaths.

We looked at one another, and we looked at the park, and we looked at one another again. Jodi squeezed my hand, and her eyes were brighter than the streetlight across the way.

Without a word being spoken between us, we both turned as one and strolled into the park. We had half an hour before we were to return to the others. Half an hour would surely be sufficient. In fact, the condition I was in, an hour would be *more* than sufficient.

We strolled along the footpath, passing a bench to our right, two trees to our left, shrubbery to our right—

We turned right.

It was pitch black in there. Twigs crackled underfoot, bushes tugged at our knees and entrapped our ankles, a low-hanging tree branch brushed my face with coarse leaves. Jodi held my hand clenched tight in hers, and in all that blackness the only thing I could see was the bright gleam of her eyes, and above the thunder of our passage I could hear her breathing, as loud and irregular as my own.

We blundered and crashed our way into the shrubbery and came, all at once, to a cleared spot, completely encircled. Jodi whispered "Whew!" and immediately sat down. I flopped down beside her, reached for her, kissed her, and we toppled backward, lying prone on the barren ground.

Active hands, active hands. We were still in our bathing suits, and I had the straps of her suit unhooked and the top half folded down, and I was doing all sorts of interesting things to her bare and beautiful breasts, when the cop suddenly put in his appearance.

He shone a flashlight on us, the blasted Peeping Tom, the beam centered on Jodi's tanned and pink-tipped breasts and she screamed. I didn't blame her, I felt like screaming myself.

I was blinded by the light at first, but then I could make out the shadowy form leaning over the bushes on the side opposite the direction of our entry. As I peered trying to make out who or what this was, a voice said, rather gruffly and much too loudly, "What's going on here?" So I knew that it had to be an officer of the law. Anyone else would have *known* what was going on there. And had the decency not to interrupt.

The long and the short of it is that Jodi and I—her top half once again barely covered by the bathing suit—were bundled into what Ylicaw apparently considered a prowl car (a dilapidated Chevy, three or four years old) and driven away to what Ylicaw apparently considered a police headquarters (a dilapidated brick structure, perhaps a hundred years old), where a short fat bald man with a red face and a red head threatened us with all sorts of unlikely punishments, grumbled at us, and wrote endlessly on sheet after sheet of paper.

Jodi, wearing only her bathing suit, carried, of course, neither money nor identification. I, however, as supply sergeant of our scouting party, had tucked my wallet into the waist of my bathing suit, and so I had identification and eight dollars. The bald man—a desk sergeant or some such thing, I suppose—took my wallet with claws that snatched, and wrote my name and home address down at least half a dozen times. I gave him a phony name for Jodi—what the name was I have no idea, at this late date—and he lectured and threatened and grumbled at us for a while again, finally releasing us with a warning to leave town at once.

By then, it was midnight. We walked, we hoped, toward the Ylicaw stadium, found it at last and, to our dismay, discovered that the cars were gone. We learned the next day that the others hadn't even noticed our non-appearance. There were ten of them, all somewhat high, and with that number in that condition it was easy to lose track of two people.

For a few minutes, we didn't know what to do. My eight dollars wasn't enough to get us back to campus, not even by bus, assuming we could find a route—changing buses, changing buses, changing buses—that would take us from the nondescript out-of-the-way dinky little hick town of Ylicaw to the equally nondescript out-of-the-way dinky little hick town where the campus was situated. At any rate, we couldn't afford a bus anyway. And it was too far to walk, of course. And far too late at night to hitchhike, on the secondary and tertiary roads that would be our inevitable route.

Jodi suggested calling someone on campus, preferably one of those who had so unceremoniously just dumped us here, at the edge of beyond. But of course we couldn't expect them to get back to the dorms before three at the earliest. In the morning, I could call someone to come and get us, but for the moment we were stuck.

The long and short of it was that we were going to have to spend the night in Ylicaw.

We talked around the subject for a few minutes and finally brought it out into the open. We were going to have to spend the night in Ylicaw.

Now, what with piercing flashlights and threatening fat men and being abandoned by our friends and whatnot, we had pretty well lost the fervor that had driven us all day long. We were neither passionate anymore, nor were we coy. And so when we spoke of staying the night here, we discussed the subject with clinical coldness.

We couldn't very well sleep in the park; neither of us was in a particular hurry to meet the flashlight-bearing patrolman or his red-faced superior again. And, dressed only in bathing suits, carrying no luggage, and with no ring on Jodi's third-finger-left-hand, staying at a hotel seemed a remote possibility. Nor were we particularly happy about the idea of spending the next nine or ten hours wandering around the streets. We were somewhat tired from our day's exertions.

We strolled, talking it over, irritated and worried. We strolled for perhaps fifteen minutes and then we saw the hotel.

It was the western edge of town. Every town in the country has a section like this, on one edge which is neither fringe nor outskirt but seems to be a small hunk of downtown broken off and rolled into a corner. A few seedy-looking stores, some equally seedy offices, and, down at the corner there, a rambling structure two stories high, fronted by a neon sign reading BAR-HOTEL.

"I'm going to take a chance," I said, the minute I saw that sign. "Places like that usually aren't too particular."

"I'll wait here," she said, tiredly.

And so she waited there. I continued down to the corner and stepped into the bar. A hotel like this, of course, had no lobby.

I made quite a stir in the bar. There were six or seven locals, hulks in hunting jackets, draped over beers at the bar, while another hulk, this one in a filthy white shirt and apron, played bartender in front of them. And here I walked in, a nineteen-year-old kid in a bathing suit.

They watched me, with stoic interest, and I got a bad case of stage fright. I sidled to the bar, the bartender ambled over, and I said—whispered, rather, for I was completely intimidated by the surroundings—"Have you a room?"

"Sure I got rooms," he said. He looked me up and down, slowly, looked beyond me through the fly-specked window at the empty street, and said, "Single or double?"

My hesitation should have been a dead giveaway. Finally, I said, "Single."

He didn't seem to notice the hesitation at all. He simply nodded and told me the charge was three dollars, and that he wanted it in advance, since I had no luggage. I paid him, gratefully, and he came out from behind the bar and led the way to my room.

We went through a door in the side wall, coming into a long narrow hall, with a street door at one end and a flight of stairs at the other. The bartender pointed at the stairs. "Up there," he said. "First door on your right." He handed me the key.

I thanked him, in a frightened whisper, and he nodded and started back to his bartending duties, pausing to look at me and point at the street door. "Bring her through there," he said. "And try to keep it quiet." Then he went back into the bar, closing the door after him.

After only a few seconds of paralysis, I raced to the street door, opened it, and waved frantically at Jodi. She came down the street at a half-trot, and when she reached me I whispered, "We've got a room. It's okay, the bartender's on our side."

"I've got to get off my feet," was all she said.

We hurried upstairs and into our room.

This time, there was no caressing, there was no physical play. We entered the room—a small barren linoleum-floored monstrosity with bed and dresser and chair—and the both of us immediately stripped off our bathing suits and crawled into bed. I switched off the light, a glaring overhead affair, and Jodi and I lay together in the dark, almost touching, but a million miles apart.

We lay there, side by side, unmoving, for perhaps fifteen minutes, and then Jodi exhaled in a long sibilant sigh and whispered, "My God, it feels good to lie down."

"This sure turned into a mess," I answered. I was beginning to feel very sorry for myself.

"Poor Harvey," she murmured. She rolled over on her side—demonstrating, in the process, that we were aboard a bed with a particularly virulent squeak—and patted my arm consolingly. "Fate was against us," she whispered.

"I'm sorry about that thing in the park," I said.

"Hush. It wasn't your fault."

"Damn it, Jodi."

"Poor Harvey," she whispered again, and leaned over to kiss me on the cheek. When she did so, her breast brushed my arm, hard and electric.

Passion, in a manner of speaking, came back in a rush.

Squeak! went the bed, as I flipped over onto my side and gathered Jodi into my arms. *Squeak!* it went again, as she pressed herself close against me, and then all was silence as we kissed, kissing with lips and tongues and hands and pushing bodies.

The feel of her beneath my hand, her breasts crushed against my chest, her hair around my face, drove me in seconds to the same fever pitch that had originally taken me all afternoon to work up. I kissed her, caressed her body, and she responded like the passionate nymph she was.

Squeak! went the bed as I pushed her over onto her back again, and *squeak!* it went once more, as I followed, moving at her and *squeak!* and *squeak!* and *squeak!* and *squeaksqueaksqueaksqueak* . . .

Long and painful as the frustration of the afternoon and evening and night had been, I was suddenly grateful for it. If I had been able to take Jodi at once, this afternoon, right off the bat, it would have been fast and furious and finished before barely begun. Even had our commingling in the park been consummated, it wouldn't have been the love that lasts. But the day's events had temporarily aged my body somewhat. No longer the randy rooster, picapicapica*puc,* I was now a mighty javelin in my very first marathon mating.

The sweat started from us, our bodies were slick and hot in the dark on the wrinkling sheets. Jodi, but eighteen then, was even less experienced than I, and at first she simply lay passive, receiving me, but the force of the rhythm awoke her body, and all at once she surged beneath me, and the bed screamed, and she moved as lustily as I. Her moaning gasping breath was hot in my ear, her arms clutched my back, her body drove and drove. Like a rolling liner on the rolling sea we rolled together.

I felt her passion climbing, up and up, and knew myself to still be strong, and knew I would last, and when she went rigid beneath me, nails sunk in the flesh of my back, legs straining upward, head arched back, I only drove harder and harder and harder still, and it wasn't till the second time for her that I finally surged to immobility, and held my breath, and squeezed my eyes shut, and bit the soft flesh of her shoulder.

We lingered together, calming slowly, our breathing gradually becoming more normal, and at last I moved over to my own side of the bed again, and Jodi kissed me, and we fell asleep in one another's arms.

We awoke late the next morning, both ravenous. We left the bar-hotel, had breakfast together at a diner, and I called one of our compatriots from last night, who promised to drive out for us at once. While waiting, Jodi and I, incredibly conspicuous on the quiet streets of Ylicaw in our bathing suits, strolled and window-shopped and held hands and, whenever no one could see us, touched one another in fond reminiscence.

Our driver, apologizing profusely for last night's oversight—for which we were, of course, no longer *angry*—arrived at about two in the afternoon, and drove us back. We had already worked out our story, and told everyone that we had been picked up by the police for wandering around in bathing suits in the park at midnight, and had spent the night in separate cells in the local hoosegow. Jodi told all her girlfriends that, and I told the same story to all the guys in the dormitory. But I, in my telling, made damn sure no one was going to believe me. Jodi was too lovely a conquest, too desirable a bedmate, for me, at callow and loud-mouthed nineteen, to be able to keep it all a secret . . .

Talking together now, Jodi more desirable and more exciting than ever in that green knit dress with the revealed expanse of thigh, we laughed over that first time, and Jodi said, "In a way, I'm glad the cop caught us. That bed was a lot softer than the ground in the park." She gave me a melting smile. "And you were a lot firmer."

Chapter 2

If Helen had been waiting for me, preferably nervous and dynamically concerned, I could at least have permitted myself the luxury of delicious guilt feelings. But such luck was not to be mine. The train let me off and the chrome-plated ranch wagon was waiting for me, emptily metallic. I turned a key in it and drove along tree-lined streets to our little hate-nest among the crab grass. I buried the car in the carport—garages are sadly out of style; all that space to waste on cars that don't fit in them anyway—and I walked around to look at the outside of our deluxe split-level colonial.

There is something reassuringly schizoid about a split-level to begin with. Ours looks as though it couldn't possibly continue to exist if the various floors were level all across the board. The imbalance of its design is essential if it's going to survive all the concentrated imbalance of the people who live in it. But when you take this split-level and make it colonial as well—colonial, for the love of the lord—well, the result is nice to visit, but wouldn't you just *hate* to live there?

The other car, Detroit's most recent attempt to barrelhouse into the compact field, was missing. It stood to reason that Helen was missing as well. She never goes anywhere without the car—in fact I was once thinking of buying her a bicycle to get into the house from the carport—and by extension the car never goes anywhere without her. I rang the bell anyway, sort of for the hell of it. If a doorbell rings and there's nobody in the house, did it really ring? It really rang. I heard it. Then I opened the door with my key and went inside.

Experience told me to go first to the kitchen. It's an electric kitchen, of course. Electric range, electric icebox, electric garbage disposal, electric washing machine, electric dishwasher, electric frying pan, electric sink, electric pop-up toaster. The sad thing is that if you put your head in the oven you can't turn on the gas. You can only turn on the electricity. Shocking, but harmless.

The kitchen had a pegboard. It came with the kitchen, of course, and it is a huge flattened-out cork shaped like a kidney where husbands and wives leave notes for each other. A last-ditch attempt at eliminating conversation forever from the domestic scene. I looked at the pegboard and there, of course, was a note from Helen.

Harv—it began, quaintly enough. *Couldn't wait dinner for you. The girls are playing at Betty's tonight. You know the number if something comes up.* Now what in the world could come up? I pushed onward. *There's a TV dinner in the fridge. Just pop it on the stove and eat hearty.* The note was unsigned but I had a fairly sound idea who had written it.

I opened the fridge and stared thoughtfully at the TV dinner. It was a Dexter Frozen Dinner. A Square Deal on a Square Meal, I thought. And just how square could you get? It was unsettling. I was selling my own wife.

I took out the TV dinner, the Dexter Frozen Dinner thought-fully provided by Harvey Christopher's Frozen Wife. I put it on the electric range and turned the dial. The burner unit glowed like neon. I looked at Dexter's creation—pieces of unhappy chicken swimming with leaden wings through a sea of à la king. I watched the green peas in one section of the aluminum foil container grow slowly warm. The frozen French fries thawed and heated.

When the chicken bubbled the dish was prepared. Scientific eating. Scientific cooking. I took the container—dishes are a waste of time, of course, even with an electric dishwasher to care for them, and besides you can only get them in boxes of soap, and soap makes too many suds and is harmful to your new automatic, and—I took the container into the family-style living room carpeted protectively from wall to wall to hide the bad job they'd done on the floor, and I sat down in a chair no more comfortable than it looked. I placed the container on the arm of the chair, then flicked the remote switch that clued in the television set to the fact that someone, by God, was eating a TV dinner, and while the set woke up and came to life I plunged a fork into the chicken mess and brought it to my mouth. I chewed it—it wasn't really necessary, because the Dexterino people sort of chew the food *for* you, scientifically, of course, as an unbeatable aid to digestion. A western was happening on the screen. I studied it for a moment, pausing before attempting another forkful of Dexter's Death Warmed Over.

And I thought about Jodi, and bed with Jodi, and Jodi's happy apartment on Lexington in the very heart of Madcap Manhattan. Jodi's apartment was not schizoid. It didn't even have a sunken living room. It was all on one level, as, for that matter, was Jodi.

And something happened. I reached for the remote switch and killed the television set in the middle of a howdy. I stood up, slowly but quite firmly, and I carried the Dexter's Frozen Tundra to the bathroom.

The toilet wasn't electric but it tried. I poured the TV dinner into it. There was no chain to pull, no handle to yank. There was instead a pedal on the floor. I trod lightly upon the pedal and the toilet gurgled pleasantly at me while Dexter's Frozen Folderol disappeared to wherever bad food goes when it dies.

I had a shaker of martinis mixed before I remembered that I didn't really like martinis. I poured them down the toilet and pedaled the pedal. It was damned enjoyable. Then I looked for the Scotch, and we were out of it. I started for the carport, stopped suddenly, and returned to the kitchen. I scrawled a note for Helen *Hel*—it began. *Went out for Scotch. Couldn't wait until you got home.* I didn't sign it, because I figured she would know who it was from.

Then I got into the ranch wagon and pointed it at Manhattan. I didn't really have to do much more than that. The car knew the way. I pointed it, and I let it drive, which it did very well with its automatic transmission and its power steering and its power brakes and its power windows and power doors. And while we rode along, the car and I, I thought about Jodi some more, and about me. My mind must have been as properly primed as the car. The memories flowed easily . . .

It was a strange affair, if you could call it an affair. I don't think you could. *Affair* means several things, and none of the things is what we had. *Affair* means contemporary adultery, or it means modern people having a go at it, or it means a Radcliffe girl having a mad fling before she marries a stockbroker's son. And Jodi and I were none of these things, so what we had wasn't really an affair, evidently.

But whatever it was, it was fine with me. We were at college, and we were young, and there is no better time nor place for falling happily and heedlessly into the hay. We were at college, and we were young, and we were not in love, and we realized this.

After the wonderful night in the wonderful hotel, after the wonderful leading up to it and the wonderful doing it and the wonderful lying there and thinking about it, there was a period of about a week during which I avoided Jodi. No, that's not it, not quite. I didn't avoid her like the plague, or walk away when I saw her coming, or steer clear of her favorite haunts. I simply made no attempt to seek her out. Our paths did not cross by accident and I did not cause them to cross by design.

I suppose I was shy, or embarrassed, or merely young. It was the way my mind worked at that period of my life. I had made love to Jodi, and it had been more fun than a beer-drinking contest, but it was over. Make love to her again? Hell, man, I already *did!* Why do it again, for God's sake?

Fear of foreign alliances, perhaps, or fear of rejection, or just stupidity. But I went on with classes and beer and rides and assorted nonsense, and I dated a few girls and caressed their breasts. Their breasts were nice, if not quite so nice as Jodi's. And at that stage of my life, the skirt of one girl was much the same as the skirt of another. If something was missing with those other girls I was barely conscious of it. Something *was* missing, of course. I didn't get to sleep with them. But I would, in due time, and I was busy making plans.

Then I ran into Jodi. Quite literally, as a matter of fact. I was strolling down the campus oblivious to mostly everything, and so was she. I didn't see her coming and I don't know whether she saw me or not, but we bumped chests, always a nice way to say hello. She started to topple over and I grabbed her and hoisted her upright again and we looked deeply into one another's eyes. I remember feeling very ashamed of myself and not knowing why.

"Harvey," she said. "I've missed you."

There was not much to say, so I mulled bashfully and took her arm. "Buy you a beer," I suggested.

"Wine," she said.

The liquor store in the silly little town closed at dusk. "I don't have any wine," I said. "And it's too late to buy any. Unless you want to go to the bar." I left the rest unsaid. You didn't go to the bar for anything but beer. If you had hard liquor you were a lush. If you had wine you were obviously trying too hard. So the hell with it.

"I have wine," she said, "In my room."

"Fine. Where will we drink it?"

"In my room."

I thought that one over. It was against the rules, a boy and a girl in a dormitory room, but so, for that matter, was a love bout in a faraway hotel. As seems to be usual, the rules of the college had little connection with reality. But, since the fundamental rule was *Don't get caught,* this being a Spartan sort of a college, and since we stood a great chance of getting caught in her room, I was a little bit worried.

"We'll get caught," I said.

She tossed her head, sort of, and looked every inch a queen. I mean it. There was something regal about her, something I should have been able to notice long ago. It was an air that said that she not only didn't give a warmed-over damn for the rules but that the punishment was equally unimportant to her. A sound attitude. One that I, unfortunately, was unable to carry off.

"If they catch us," I said, "they'll give us the old heave-ho. We won't graduate."

"So what?"

"You need a diploma," quothe I, "to be a success."

"At what?"

I wondered at what, since I had not made up my mind just what I was going to be a success at. There was a cartoon once which summed things up—a guidance counselor studying a small boy, both counselor and boy wearing thick glasses. *But Arnold,* said the caption, plaintively, *it's not enough to be a genius. You have to be a genius AT something.* That was I, with *success* instead of *genius.* I was majoring, theoretically, in English, which meant that I read books instead of tables. But I didn't want to be a writer or a reader or, God save us, a professor.

"At something," I said to Jodi.

"If you come up to my room," she said, "and if we drink the wine there, you are going to be a success. At something. At something that's fun." And she stepped so close to me that I could feel her. We were smack dab in the middle of the campus, and there were probably people around, and I did not care. Her breasts bumped into me and I remembered them—in the water, in the bed, firm and lovely in my hands. She did something with her hips, sort of throwing them at me. And I remembered things that were very nice to remember.

I looked at her. She was in uniform—sweater and skirt, saddle shoes. I looked at her and sweater and skirt melted away in a dissolve no Hollywood studio could attempt to duplicate. I saw a naked Jodi in Technicolor and cinemascope. She bounced at me again and naked breasts banged into me, naked hips offered themselves.

I had nothing to say. But I had things to do. I took her arm in my arm, possessive as a papa bear, and off we went to the little dormitory room that she called home.

"The best way," she said, "is nonchalance. We'd better not try to sneak in. If we do, somebody will see us, and we'll look sneaky. That's no good."

That sounded reasonable enough.

"But if we walk in as though we have every reason in the world to be there," she went on, "we'll look natural enough. They'll think we're studying together or something."

"We will be."

She giggled a charming giggle. "Studying," she mused. "It's a shame. I mean, you ought to get a diploma for it. If you're good enough."

"So you think you'd be good enough?" Remember, she was less experienced than I was. Not many people could have made that statement. So here, for a change, I was the Voice of Authority, the old man on the mountain, the accomplished lecher teaching the young prodigy how to get ahead on a horizontal basis.

"Practice," she said, "makes perfect."

"So let's practice."

Her room was on the third floor of the sterile brick dormitory. She led the way and up the stairs we went. A girl met us, stopped to chat. We chatted amiably about something or other. And, incredibly, it was working. The girl noticed me, all right. And there I was, leading the lovely Jodi up the primrose stairway, and there was this girl, noticing the fact and thinking nothing of it. Nonchalance, then, was the ticket.

Then we were in the room. Jodi, happily, did not have a roommate. She barely had a room. It was the single, the room the architects had made a mistake about, the little cubicle crouched precariously across the narrow hall from the community bathroom. The room had a bed, sort of, and a dresser, and an excuse for a closet. The dresser and the closet were unnecessary for the time being. The bed was there—inviting, beckoning—and we were there—hungry, eager—and the wine was there, red and sour.

"I really would like some wine," she said. "Unless you're in a hurry."

There was something strange about that line. We were there to make love, you see, and her attitude was that, while she'd like to sip Chianti and talk for a moment or two, she'd be perfectly willing to stretch out on the rack if I was in a rush. Generosity? No, more than that. Here was a girl who understood the place of woman in the total scheme of things. Here was a girl who knew the proper position of woman in the social order.

"Let's have some wine, then."

"We'll have to drink it out of the bottle."

I said that was fine, and she yanked out the cork, and she took a drink. She could drink magnificently. I watched with mute admiration while the level of wine in the bottle went steadily down.

Then she passed the bottle to me. I almost wiped off the neck instinctively, the way you always do when someone hands you a bottle, but I remembered that I was going to make love to this girl in a minute or two and there didn't seem to be much point in such health precautions. I drank, taking as much as she had taken, and passed the bottle back to her.

She finished it and heaved it at the wastebasket. It missed and struck first the wall and then the floor. It bounced twice on the floor before it cracked, and when it cracked it did not fool around. It shattered into splintered glass.

"Damn," she said thoughtfully. "We'd better not go barefoot. Not over there, anyhow."

She turned to me. We were sitting on the edge of that very narrow bed, and when she turned to me I took her in my arms and I kissed her. It was not one of those kisses that sent a striking bolt of passion shooting through the last atom of one's being. It was a much more contemplative sort of kiss. She was there, and I was there too, and our mouths were together and it was nice.

Her lips parted and my tongue stole past them like a thief in the night.

The kiss was long. It was one of those slow kisses that let us think over and decide that everything was going very well indeed. The kiss ended and she stood up. She peeled the sweater over her head. She was not wearing a bra, and it was just as well, because if she had been I would have torn the damned thing off of her. She did not need a bra—it would have been like harnessing a whirlwind. The whirlwind was unharnessed and my hands reached for cool soft flesh. Her nipples were buds a-blooming.

"That's nice," she said. "Very nice. When you stroke them and like that. It feels good." There was something detached about her words and about the way she said them, as if she were carefully taking stock of just what I was doing and just how good it felt. I bent down and put one of those nipples to lips and she very suddenly stopped talking. Her muscles went tense and then her body began to move with something that had to be passion.

"Let me take everything off," she said. "All my clothes. Then we can fool around for a while and then we can do it. But I don't want to mess my skirt."

"Fine," I said. It may well go down in history as the understatement of the century.

She got undressed. Rather, the skirt flowed off of her, and the panties flowed off of her, and the silly saddle shoes fell from her feet, and the socks followed them, and everything that I was looking at belonged to Jodi, and consequently to me as well.

"You like?"

A silly question.

"Now you get undressed, Harvey. I want to watch. Unless you're bashful."

If I was, I decided, I could get over it. I felt a wee bit self-conscious stripping my clothes off, especially the way she stared at me with a cross between curiosity and desire, but I managed.

"You like?" I asked. I had to say *something*.

"Mmmmmm."

And then toppled we to the bed, as Time might put it. And then kissed we, as backward rolled sentences while whirled the mind. And then fondled we, and stroked me, and touched we, and then, whee!

"Harvey—"

I wondered what she wanted.

"Harvey, do you have a thing?"

I was lost.

"So I won't get a baby," she said.

"Oh."

"Because that wouldn't be any good. Getting a baby, I mean. Inconvenient."

I did not have a thing. For weeks I had carried one around in my wallet, just as most college students do. But, sad to say, I had used it. Before I met Jodi. Before I got next to Jodi, anyway. And, thinking about it, I had an unhappy thought.

"Last time—"

She was right there with me. "Last time," she said, "there was nothing to worry about. But—"

"I don't have one."

"Then we can't do it."

That was something to ponder. "We can start to," I said thoughtfully. "And before anything happens, we can stop, and then—"

"A friend of mine did that."

"Yeah? What happened?"

"She had a baby."

"Oh," I said hollowly. "Then . . . do you want to wait while I . . . uh . . . find a drugstore?"

Alarm was an ugly black shadow across her pretty face. "That will take too long," she said. "I couldn't possibly wait. It would tear me apart."

I had to admit that I couldn't wait either. The dilemma grew. And grew. And grew.

"Harvey," she said plaintively. "Harvey, there is a way. I . . . you might not like it. I mean, it's not . . . some people would say it isn't normal. If that makes a difference. But I wouldn't get a baby that way."

I asked her what way she meant and she told me.

Is there anyone in the world so prudish as a college boy? The young lotharic type, out to conquer the female half of the universe, is in his own weak way as puritanical as any spinster from here to Bessarabia. If they have spinsters in Bessarabia. And I was quite roundly shocked.

But I was also quite roundly ready, and it was easier to conceal the shock than the evidence of my interest in Jodi. So I reached for her, playing the scene by ear as it were, and it began.

It was her first time at that particular fun-and-games method, but she took to it like a mallard to hydrous oxide, and away we went, off into outer space. It was good, and it was fun, and Jodi's particular brand of Scotch was chosen forever.

I spent the night with her. Ill-advised, in a way—any damned fool could have wandered into her little room and loused things up for both of us as far as the college was concerned. But I was unable to see myself tiptoeing out of the girl's dorm at three in the morning. Nonchalance is only good for so long. Then the roof falls in on you.

So we topped the world by being a bit much in the line of nonchalance. We slept, body to body, and when we woke up the idea of her getting pregnant seemed far less important, and we risked it. Then she went off to breakfast, bringing me a very modest repast in a paper bag, and we crawled back in the sack for another go at it.

I left that dorm at high noon and no one looked at me twice.

Youth. She didn't get pregnant from that delightful evening. And after that I was careful, very careful. And, for some reason which eluded me then but which was very important nevertheless, my conquest became a secret one. I suppose it was Jodi's change in status from conquest to partner. We were having an affair, not playing a seduction scene. There was no need to ply her with liquor, to woo her with words of love, to con her in one perverse way or another. There was no need to do anything but ask her, and that was enough.

I was clever and conscientious. I kept up-to-date in my scholastic endeavors, such as they were. I slept alone, confining our amours to an hour here and an hour there. I worked at my books and I gave her the hours that were left, because school was important and the future, the glowing shiny chrome-plated future, it was more important. And Jodi—well, Jodi was important, too, because Jodi was a valuable outlet and a pleasant way to spend an hour here and an hour there. But Jodi was not important enough.

"It's a shame," she said, one afternoon on a blanket on the golf course—a common abode of lovers; no one in the history of the college ever committed the cardinal sin of playing *golf* there, for the love of God—"that you don't love me. And that I don't love you."

"Why?"

"I don't know," she said, dreamily, her hand doing magical things. "I don't know, exactly. Except that I think it would be nice."

"Love," I said. "Nice."

"Kind of."

I put my hand inside her blouse and felt a nipple stiffen. I caressed and she purred. I put another hand up her skirt and she gasped. Not a gasp of surprise and not a gasp of passion but something harder to define. As if she was thrilled by the fact that I was touching her and that she was responding, and wasn't it nice?

It was that. And the afternoon was a trip to the moon on the gossamerest of wings, and, in the words of the bard, the world moved. No sleeping bag, but you can't have everything.

She remembered the next day. "Love," she said.

"Love," I said. "Moon and June. Do you know that there are only four words in the English language that rhyme with love?" I told her erroneously.

She hadn't known that.

"Glove, dove, shove and above," I said. "Want to write a poem? Sing a song?"

She didn't. She wanted to be somber. "I don't think I'll ever fall in love," she said. "I'd like to, kind of. But I don't think it will ever happen to me."

It was the regal Jodi speaking, the far-off look in the lovely eye. One did not speak when the queen spoke. One listened thoughtfully and hung on every word.

"Some women are made for love," she said, "and some are not. I'm made for sex, I guess. Or something like that. But not for love."

"How can you tell?"

The spell was broken the mood shattered. Wherever she had been, she was there no longer. "Let's make love," she said happily.

"Or let's make sex. Let's make something, for goodness sake, and let's do it as well as we possibly can." Which was very well indeed . . .

I garaged the car, not wanting to carry the memory any further. It had carried me as far as Manhattan and that was quite far enough. Any more would be bad, because the only course for memory to follow was the course of an affair that went downhill from there in a way I did not enjoy reminiscing about. And after that there were ten more years of my life to consider, and the less I considered them, the better.

So I garaged the car and paid the man and walked into Manhattan. I don't know what I was looking for, exactly, except that I was thirsty. The bar I found was on 47th Street between Fifth and Madison. It was late, businesswise, but the boys were still there.

I heard phrases that I didn't want to listen to. I heard the fey patter and the unhip hipness, and I drank Vat 69 and did not talk to anybody. I was roundly bored, and the only thing that could have been more boring was the little split-personality home in Rockland County, with or without my barren witch aboard to louse things up.

The liquor was good and I drank quite a bit of it. I'd had no dinner, of course—just a mouthful of Dexter's Deflavored Dishwater—and I still had a little of the edge from the Scotch I'd shared with Jodi. And the more I drank the more sploshed I got, and the more sploshed I got the less I wanted to spend the evening sitting in an ad man's bar.

I left the place, left the unasked-for twist of lemon curling around the rim of my glass, and I walked. I did not know where I was going.

I was actually surprised when I found out that I was on Lexington Avenue. Surprised, but not confused. Lexington rang its bell at once and I knew where I was and why, and I only hoped she wasn't busy with a customer.

I stopped for a drink on the way. Then I stopped again, this time in a liquor store, and I asked the clerk for a bottle of Vat 69. He gave it to me and took my money and I waltzed out into the street again.

The desk clerk at her hotel called her on the phone. "Let me talk to him," she must have said, because he presented me with the receiver and I held it to my ear.

"Harvey," she said, sounding pleased. Her voice was a throaty whisper. "Honey, can you come back in half an hour? Or forty-five minutes, that would be better. I'm busy right now, honey, but forty-five minutes—"

I found a bar for the forty-five minutes. I felt silly, paying bar prices for liquor with a paper bag full of better liquor at my foot. I felt even sillier, waiting for three quarters of an hour to see a girl I'd seen that afternoon, waiting until my friend, who happened to be a whore, got rid of her guest, who could only be a customer. I drank a little more than I'd planned on drinking and when I left the bar and returned to the hotel, exactly forty-five minutes after I had talked to her, I was pretty well stoned.

The desk clerk recognized me, called up, spoke softly for a moment or three, and gave me the nod. The elevator took me to her floor and her door was open, her face smiling at me.

"Harvey," she said, looking at me oddly. "Is something wrong, baby?"

"Long time no see," I muttered vacantly. I poured myself into her room and her arms swallowed me.

Chapter 3

I was twenty-two. A lovely age to be; I hadn't been twenty-two for years. *How many years? No, no, that required counting, and counting hurt the head, and there was the dim possibility I would wake up. Voices murmured.*

Back, back, back down into unconsciousness. Where was I? I was twenty-two.

Yes, that's it. I was twenty-two, and it was summer. Oh, my *God,* was it summer! It was summer like the inside of an oven, which one shared with the biggest klieg light of them all. Too hot and too bright, and the humidity was fantastic. The air was about eighty percent water; one didn't walk down the street, one did the breaststroke. And that's the only kind of breaststroke one did; it was much too hot for any other kind, and besides that I was living at the Y.

That's it! I was twenty-two, and it was summer, and it was New York, and I was living at the Y. "I'm going to New York after graduation," I said to everybody. "But I hear it's awful expensive to live in New York. I don't know what to do about an apartment." And everybody said. "Live at the Y. It's cheap, and it's clean." So I lived at the Y.

And nobody told me I was going to be pawed surreptitiously all the time. And in that heat, too. All these heavy-breathing dark-eyed boys prowling the clean cheap halls at the Y, panting. They were the only things around hotter than the sidewalks.

And the sidewalks were hot. I walked on them, and the bottoms of my shoes got hot. And then I walked some more, and the bottoms of my feet got hot. And then my feet, which were encased by shoes, got hot. And then my ankles got hot. And then I walked into a bar and sat down at a table, because I couldn't take my shoes off if I sat on a stool at the bar, and I spent a dime of what was left of my savings on a glass of draft, and I sat holding the cold glass in both hands and wiggling my toes. I was twenty-two, and despite it all it was delicious to be alive.

A man came over to my table. It was three-thirty in the afternoon, there were only about eight or nine people in the entire bar, and this man came over to my table. He wasn't one of the ones like at the Y, he was one of the ones like at the bar, gray-suited and somber-faced, with twenty-year-old bodies and thirty-year-old faces and forty-year-old jowls and fifty-year-old appetites for booze.

This man came over to my table. "You've got your shoes off," he said.

I was twenty-two and my shoes were off and it was delicious to be alive. "By God, sir," I said, "you are absolutely right."

"I think that's great," he said. He wasn't drunk, but then he wasn't sober either. He waved a hand that more or less held a glass containing an amber fluid and two clear unfogged ice cubes with holes in their tummies. "I think that's absolutely great," he said, expanding on his last remark, and added, "Mind if I sit down?"

"By all means, sir," I said. I was twenty-two, and I called everyone over twenty-five 'sir,' because that's the way I was brought up, buddy.

He sat down, lowered the glass to the black Formica table top, and leaned forward to study me, one might say, piercingly. After too long a time of this activity, he straightened up, leaned forward again, and said, "You married?"

"Not as yet," I said, so there would be no misunderstanding.

"Hah!" he cried, and sloshed drink on the Formica. "I knew it," he announced. "The minute I looked at you, and I saw your shoes was off—were off—I said to myself, 'There is a free man. That man over there with his shoes off is not married to anybody at all, not even once.' That's what I said to myself."

"You converse rather well," I complimented him. God, it was *delicious* to be alive!

"Do you want to know something?" he asked me. Accepting my millisecond of silence for consent, he hastened on. "I have been coming into this bar every afternoon," he announced, adding parenthetically and inaccurately, "at the coffee break, for the last eight years. Summer, winter, hot weather, rainy weather, *all* of that stuff. And do you want to know something?"

"Something else?" I asked him.

"I have never," he said emphasizing his words by rhythmically sloshing drink in the general neighborhood, "never in all that time seen anyone in here take off his shoes. What do you think of that?"

"Not much," I said.

"Exactly!" he cried.

At that moment, a waiter came by. I could tell he was a waiter by the filthy apron wrapped round his middle. Everything else in the bar, including the bartender, the customers, the glasses, the tables and the floor, all were clean, except this dour-faced man in his rape-of-Troy apron. "You can't have your shoes off in here," is what he said to me.

I had just about decided that my shoes were getting a lot more attention than they deserved. They were just a cheap pair of old black shoes. I'd worn them for three years now, practically all the way through college. Not to bed, of course, but almost always else.

The man opposite me said, "Never mind," to the waiter.

The waiter looked at him, and then looked questioningly at the bartender over there, and the bartender shook his head in a leave-them-alone gesture, and I knew at once that I was talking to an Important Man, and I thought of all the success stories I knew which opened in bars, but practically all of them were sexual, so I dropped that line of thought. I was living in the Y, and it had been five weeks since I had last seen Jodi, and there was little likelihood I would ever see her again, and I hadn't yet found a job so that I could have an apartment and meet girls and start all over again with someone else, so I did my level best not to even think about sex. The heat helped, that way.

The Important Man then said, "What's your line, my friend?"

"I don't have one yet," I admitted. "I came to New York three weeks ago," I explained, "armed with my brand-new sheepskin, and I've been prowling the streets, turning down management-trainee jobs, ever since."

"Good," he said. "What kind of college? You an engineer or something? Or what?"

Did I look like an engineer? "It was a Liberal Arts College," I said, rather stiffly, "and quite a good one at that, where I obtained a Bachelor of Arts, with a major in English, primarily American and British Literature."

"Now, what the hell," he said. He looked at me, frowning, puzzled, obviously ready and willing to learn something. "Now what the hell did you do that for?" he asked me.

I blinked. I'm sure I did. "What the hell did I do what for?" I parried.

"Get your degree," he explained patiently, "in English. Now, you could of got your degree in anything you wanted, history or science or even philosophy, and you could of been adapted into American industry, some way or another. But English? Let me tell you something, my friend. By the way, the name's Tom Stanton."

"Harvey Christopher," I told him, and we solemnly shook hands. His hand was wet. From the drink. I surreptitiously dried my hand on my trousers.

"Let me tell you something, Harv," he said, for which I never forgave him. After all, I had been calling *him* 'sir.' "It's this way," he went on, ignoring my reaction. "American industry, now, distrusts the English major. And for very good reasons, too. The English major is very liable to be a guy who thinks like mad, all the time, but what he's thinking about is very rarely much use to American industry. You see what I mean? What, do you figure to be—a writer?"

"No," I said. "Nothing like that. I would simply like to get a job in American industry. But not, frankly, any of the management trainee positions I've been offered in the last few weeks. They look very much like dead-end streets to me."

"You're right there," he said at once. "There, you are one hundred percent right. Tell me something, Harv? What do you think about advertising?"

"Advertising? I don't suppose I've ever thought much about it at all," I admitted, "except when a particularly horrendous singing commercial comes on the radio."

"Sure," he said. "But what about advertising men? You know, the scapegoats, the ones the people all the time make the funny remarks about. What about them?"

"What *about* them?" I asked him right back.

"Have you ever thought of being one?"

I hadn't. I said so, adding, "Though now that you mention it, it sounds like a good idea. After all, an English major—"

He shook his head. "English majors," he said somberly, "come to advertising agencies only long enough to soak up the atmosphere. Then they go write a nasty book. Either that, or they stay around forever and have guilt feelings, and they keep missing work and coming in the next day with a note from their psychiatrist. That's the way it is with English majors in advertising."

I considered the problem, wriggling my toes beneath the table. After due consideration, I said, "I don't think I'd be that way."

"Neither do I," he said at once. "I think you're the exception to the rule. There's an exception to every rule, you know."

"I'd heard rumors," I admitted.

"The minute I looked at you," he said, starting off on that again, "and saw you sitting there with your shoes off, I said to myself, 'There's an exception to the rule.' And I think I was right. You want a job?"

There were a million possible things to say. I said, "What?"

There were a million possible things *he* could have said, too. He said, "A job."

My keen analytical mind flashed hither and yon over our preceding conversation, correlating, comparing, combining implications, grouping subject matters, following the thin threads of cortical reasoning, and in less than a second I had the whole knotty problem doped out. "You mean," I said, "a job in advertising."

"You have," he said indistinctly, "a keen analytical mind. A job in advertising is *exactly* what I mean."

"Well," I said. "Gosh. I hadn't exactly thought much about it."

"Harv," he said with the disgusting familiarity that is so prevalent in certain otherwise-genteel sections of this city, "I'll tell you who I am. Ever heard of MGSR&S?"

I allowed as how I hadn't.

"Well," he said, "I'm S sub-two."

My keen analytical mind couldn't quite analytic that one. Apparently my mental floundering showed on my face, because he returned to English. "MGSR&S," he told me, "is Manning, Greenville, Silverstein, Rorschach and Stanton. Stanton is me."

"Ah," I said. "I see."

He looked at his watch. "Coffee break's over," he said, and engulfed the liquid in the glass. He spared the ice cubes. "Come on over to the office," he suggested, rising with surprising steadiness to his feet, "and we'll talk it over."

"Why, thank you," I said. I stood, and we started toward the door. We'd gone no more than five paces when he looked at me oddly, and said, "Don't you want your shoes?"

"Oh, yes!" I exclaimed. "My shoes!"

I went back to the table, feeling like a fool, and fished around among the crumpled cigarette packages until I found my shoes. Shod, I returned to Stanton, S sub-two. He was surveying me somewhat oddly.

I felt called upon to defend myself, albeit timidly. "It's the first time I ever forgot them," I said. It was a weak defense.

"That's all right," he said. "Come along." A bit of doubt had come into his voice. Perhaps he was growing more sober, and the prospect of hiring a man solely on the basis of him having his shoes off no longer seemed so enjoyable to him.

But I was twenty-two, and it was summer, and I was newly in New York, and the unreality of this man's conversation and job offer was of such a high level that I wasn't a bit confused or worried or nervous during the following employment interview, and I got the job.

And so I learned about advertising.

Do you know about advertising? When an otherwise-desirable young lady appears on your television screen and, to a Neanderthalic melody, sings, "Winky dinky hinky rink, Goulash beer is the beer to drink," do you have the idea that it all came out of her own little head in just a second or two? Well, you're wrong. Shakespeare wrote *Macbeth* in less time than it took a whole staff of people at MGSR&S to write those eleven words. Of course, Shakespeare had the edge. He just used English; he didn't have to *make up* exciting new words, like 'winky.'

I won't go into the entire hierarchy and nomenclature of an advertising agency, of the little bitsy contribution of every member of that crowd to the epic quoted above. I am not avoiding this naming of parts out of a fear of boring the reader, I am doing so out of a fear of boring *me*. Twelve years, let me tell you, can be a long time.

I *will* tell you however, out of an obvious bid for sympathy, what *my* contribution to that Cro-Magnon couplet was. I made it rhyme. When it came to me, the meter had already been established—though the melody hadn't yet surged out of our symphonic department—and the first line read (do you mind?), "Goulash beer is hotsy tots." I changed 'hotsy tots' to 'hinky dink.' Someone else changed the first half of the line, and altered my contribution to hinky *rink*. Whether one man added winky and one man added dinky or one man doubled up and added both words I don't know. Having contributed of my talents already, I slept through the rest of the conferences. And, at those rare conferential moments when I was awake, I wiled the time away drawing nonsensical pictures on my notepad.

Such was my job, but I didn't begin at that exalted level. Oh, no, one doesn't simply step into an important job like that. I began in the mailroom.

(*I seem to be waking up. I'd much rather not wake up; if I do my head will explode. People are talking, I can hear the murmur of their conversation distantly, and I don't imagine I want them to start talking to me. I must go back to sleep. Be twenty-two again, remember back, float back and down, back and down, find something on which to pin my floating psyche and avoid consciousness.*)

•   •   •

Laura Gray.

Ah, yes, Laura Gray. Her first name wasn't Laura, it was Natalie. And her last name wasn't Gray, it was Gregenbaum. Why is it that depressed minorities invariably express agreement with the unflattering opinions of their depressors?

At any rate I know these horrible secrets about Laura Gray because I snuck into the Personnel offices and looked at her records. I'm not sure why I did that except that I was twenty-two. And I would dearly have loved to have Laura Gray as the replacement for Jodi, and because Laura invariably cut me dead every time she saw me.

She was a secretary, Laura was. She was from the secretarial pool (I always get a picture of a bunch of laughing nude girls at a round shallow swimming pool with a statue of Cupid in the middle when I hear that phrase, don't you?) and she sat all day typing revelations granted her by a Dictaphone machine. My mailroom job consisted of distributing incoming mail all morning and picking up outgoing mail all afternoon, so I saw Laura Gray rather often, and she always cut me dead. After all, I was just a nobody from the mailroom.

Then I snuck into the Personnel office and found out her name and age and home address and other fascinating information and I went around smirking at her for a few days, and she went on cutting me just as dead as if I didn't know that she'd changed her name.

Invariably, she irked me. There finally came the day when she had irked me just a little too much, and I no longer even *wanted* her to replace Jodi. On that fateful day, out of a meanness of spirit that until then I hadn't known I possessed, I became snide with dear Laura Gray.

It was a Wednesday afternoon, and I was gathering correspondence from out baskets all over the place. I paused beside Laura's desk, looking at her as she typed glaze-eyed the orders being whispered to her by the ubiquitous Dictaphone machine, and waited for her to notice me.

She did, at last, and raised her foot from the machine pedal, cutting off its dictation. "What do *you* want?" she demanded, and there was a whole world of scorn in those four syllables.

"I was just wondering," I said, my voice as sweet as blueberry pie.

"Wondering *what?*" she snapped, with Olympian impatience.

"If it's true what they say about Jewish girls," I said.

She blinked. "*What?*"

"You know. About it being sideways."

Now, of course there were about ten thousand possible answers to that remark, any one of which would have been enough to get me fired, but I just didn't care. I was irked. So I stood blandly and waited for her answer.

Lo and behold! The color fled her face at first, but then rushed right back again, all in the space of a second. And then she *smiled!* Laura *smiled!*

And said, all trace of hostility gone from her voice, "No, silly. That's *Chinese* girls."

"Oh, go on," I said. That's all I could manage, under the circumstances.

Laura was being very arch all of a sudden, smiling coyly and generally being flirtatious as all get-out. It just goes to show you, you never know the right approach.

At any rate, we discussed anatomy a little while longer, and before I returned to the mailroom we had made a date for that very night.

There are many similarities between the young man on Madison Avenue who works in the mailroom and a young man on Madison Avenue who works as, say, an account executive. They dress in precisely the same uniform, they wear precisely the same horn-rimmed glasses, they eat precisely the same lunch in precisely the same luncheonettes, they read precisely the same magazines, and they work precisely the same hours. There is only one difference between them. The account executive earns about five times as much as the mailroom boy.

Which is simply to say that I did not take Laura Gray to the Ruban Bleu. Nor did I take her to see a Broadway show. I took her to a cheap movie theater in the Village and we saw two depressing flicks from Italy. Then I took her to a cheap coffee house, and I swear the customers were the same people we'd just seen in the movies. And then I took her home. To *her* home, I mean. I was still living at the Y. Mailroom salaries and all that.

She lived up on West 69th Street, in one of those buildings that looks as though it must have grown like a tree because nobody in the world would be idiotic enough to *build* a building that way, and I accompanied her all the way up in the elevator and to her apartment door.

Where she said, "Thank you for a lovely evening." Scarcely original.

"The evening," I said, also with scant originality, "is a pup."

"I don't hear it barking," she said.

Now, there's no possible answer to a nonsense line like that. So I didn't try to answer it. Instead, I wrapped my manly arms around her womanly body, and I kissed her.

She kissed very well. She curved against me as though she wanted to be glued in place, and her fingers played at the back of my neck, and her waist was just the perfect size for my arm.

We broke at last, and she smiled. "Thank you again," she said, her voice huskier than normal.

"Thank *you*," I said gallantly, and reached for her again.

She backed away, bumping into her apartment door. "I have to go to bed now," she said.

"Of course," I said.

"Now, Harvey," she said. "You've been a perfect gentleman all evening."

"Ridiculous," I exclaimed, stung to the quick. "Who did you think that was in the movie, the little old lady on the other side of you?"

"You know what I mean," she said, smiling again.

I coughed, not too convincingly. "I'm dying," I told her, "for a cup of coffee."

"That isn't what you're really after," she said. She was being coy again.

"Let's talk about it," I said, "while I drink the coffee."

"Well, all right."

She unlocked her door, and we went in. I drank the coffee—it was instant, and terrible—and then she started talking about me going home again. We were in the kitchen, so I merely backed her up against the refrigerator and kissed her again. She responded just as nicely as she had the last time. I was emboldened, certain that she was simply putting up token resistance, and so I started to waltz. Still kissing her, I waltzed her out of the kitchen and across the living room, headed for the bedroom beyond. But midway across the room she took the lead away from me and veered us away from the bedroom door and toward the sofa. I went along with the gag, figuring that if she wanted to make an intermediate stop it was okay with me, and we tumbled onto the sofa together, our arms still around one another and our lips still pressed firmly one to one.

When we came up for air at last, she murmured, "We shouldn't, Harv," and sort of wriggled against me.

"You're absolutely right," I told her, and unbuttoned her blouse.

We discussed the situation, amid kisses and caresses and other amusements, for about half an hour, which is to say until we were both nude. And then I suggested that it was time we went on into the bedroom.

"Harv, we shouldn't," she said, a line that was getting progressively sillier as we went along.

"At this point," I told her, "I think we absolutely should. Not only that, I think we must, if you see what I mean."

She giggled, seeing what I meant.

But she wouldn't get up from the sofa. And so, at last, I simply got to my feet, gathered her into my arms, and carried her into the bedroom, where I plopped her down on the bed during another, "Harv, we shouldn't."

Perhaps we shouldn't, but we did.

Did you ever see a fan with ribbons tied on the front grill? When the fan is turned on, the ribbons fly straight out, fluttering and jumping around like mad. Change this picture from the horizontal to the vertical, change the ribbons to arms and legs, and you have some idea what I had to contend with, once we decided to do that which we shouldn't.

Talk about explosions! Another thing those ribbons lack are claws. I was certain that by the time it was all over I was going to be black and blue everywhere except where I was clawed bright red. Very colorful, no doubt, but not too comfortable.

But such mundane thoughts cannot hold one's attention long under circumstances of that type, nor did they hold me for very long. I simply gave as good as I got, discovered that both of us enjoyed the mutual pummeling no end, and so we hurtled on across the bed to ecstasy.

When it was all over but the heavy breathing, Laura smiled at me and stroked my cheek with soft hands, and lit me a cigarette. I smoked it, contented, and Laura said, "You see? Not true at all."

"Must be the Chinese," I said.

After a while, we put our cigarettes out, turned out the light, and prepared ourselves for sleep. Shortly before sleep came, I whispered, "I'll get my things from the Y tomorrow."

She murmured, "Mmmmm." And we went to sleep . . .

. . . *Only to be awakened by somebody shaking my shoulder,* and a gruff male voice said, "Okay, buddy, you've slept it off long enough."

I tried to say, "Go away," but I think what actually came out was, "Gremmmfff."

"It's time to join the conversation, little man," said the gruff male voice.

I opened my eyes.

That was a mistake. In the first place, I wasn't twenty-two any more. In the second place, I wasn't in Laura Gray's bed anymore, I was in Jodi's bed. In the third place, I had the kind of hangover that made Grant such a surly general. And in the fourth place, there was a man I'd never seen before leaning over me, waking me up.

I'd never seen him before. Up till that moment, I hadn't known how lucky I was. Now my luck had changed.

This guy would scare little children. This guy would also scare mothers and Marines and Mau Maus. He looked like a boxer who'd lost a close decision to a meat-grinder.

"Time to join the party, little man," this apparition told me. A meaty hand descended from on high and love-tapped me on the cheek. I think it loosened teeth.

"I'm awake," I said.

"Good boy," said the monster. He backed away, saying, "Now, sit up like a good little man."

I sat up, like a good little man, to discover that I wasn't in Jodi's bed after all, I was on Jodi's sofa in Jodi's living room. And I was fully dressed, including my shoes. I had slept with my shoes on and now my feet felt like boiled turnips. All puffy and yellow.

I sat there, blinking miserably, and slowly it came home to me that I was in a *woman's* apartment, but I had been awakened by a *man*.

A husband! No, that was ridiculous, Jodi was a whore. That didn't mean she couldn't have a husband, though I didn't think she did have one, but it did mean that her husband—real or hypothetical—would stay away from her place of work.

A policeman?

Maybe I was being arrested. Maybe it was a vice raid. That was a charming thought.

I peered blearily at the monster again. He might have been a policeman—there are policemen who have that orangutan quality—but he didn't seem particularly anxious to arrest me.

Then I noticed Jodi, sitting in the armchair across the room. She was still wearing the knit green dress, and still had one leg crossed over the other to reveal all that gleaming thigh, but now she was simply sitting there, her face a careful blank as she smoked a cigarette.

"Jodi," I said. "What's going on?"

"I'm about to tell you, little man," said the monster.

Jodi didn't look at me, she looked at the monster. "Al," she said, her voice tired, as though she didn't expect any answer at all, "why don't we just leave him alone? Harvey's a nice guy."

"Am I going to hurt him?" demanded Al. I would have liked to have known the answer to that one myself.

I said, "I have to go home."

"Not just yet," said Al. He pulled over a chair and sat down in front of me. He offered me a cigarette, and when we had both lighted up he said, "Now you're a married man, am I right?"

"Yes," I said.

"And Jodi here's a whore, right?"

"Yes," I said.

He pointed the cigarette to the right. "And that thing over on the table there is a camera, right?"

I just stared at it. It had one eye, and that eye was baleful.

"Now, little man," said Al cheerfully, "I got a proposition for you."

CHAPTER 4

Now I have gone through something very much like thirty-four years of reacting incorrectly. Whenever confronted by the sort of situation in which my response ought to be thoroughly predictable, I cross up the experts and do something wrong. When I was twelve, and cooped up in a coatroom with an apprentice Lolita, a warm-blooded moppet with auburn tresses who kissed me with lips and tongue, with arms tight around me and budding breasts rampant, I was not excited, not shocked, not even taken back. I stepped away from her and asked her, solicitous as a student nurse, what brand of toothpaste she used.

I could cite other examples, but this should suffice. Take heed—I am not boasting. Perhaps there is something wrong with me, perhaps certain cerebral connections have been disconnected within my cranial cavity. I do not know, nor do I particularly care. What I *do* know, as sure as Luther Burbank made little blue apples, is that I am a perennial source of disappointment to persons who bounce supposed-to-be-shocking bits of news off me.

I disappointed Al.

There I was, disturbingly respectable, thoroughly married and gainfully employed. And there was Jodi, recently ravished. And there was this camera which had purportedly caught us *in flagrante delectable*. According to all the established rules, I was supposed to fall on my knees and beg, or race to heave the camera through the nearest open or shut window, or simply do a lap-dissolve into saline tears.

Perhaps it was the afterglow of a tumble with Jodi—which had obviously taken place, and which had undoubtedly been enjoyable, and which, damn it to hell and back, I could not recall. Perhaps it was the Vat 69, which left me with no hangover but with a delicious sense of well-being and security. Perhaps it was the elementary fact that the possible loss of my Spiritless Spouse did not terrify me. If a slew of pictures would send Helen flying to Reno, I would shed no tears. I would even supply transportation, in the form of a new broom.

So I did not fall to my knees in the manner of a sorrowful supplicant. Nor did I make a grab for the camera. Nor did I abandon my masculinity and weep.

What I said was: "Has anybody got a cigarette?"

Al didn't, or didn't care. Jodi passed me a flip-top box which I glumly recognized as an account of MGSR&S. I took one and set it aflame, sucking in smoke and expelling perfect smoke rings, wispy symbols of what Jodi meant to me. Al waited patiently, the perfect anthropoid. Jodi looked sorrowful.

Then I said: "When you print the roll, send me three copies of each shot."

I looked at Al while Jodi laughed happily somewhere in the background. I watched animal expressions play across Al's face. Any moment, I thought, he was going to hit me.

He didn't. "Look," he said. "Don't be a stupid, huh? You know what I can do with those pictures?"

"You can't sell them to the *Daily News,*" I said. "They draw the line at cheesecake. You can peddle them to school kids, I suppose, but I hear the competition is keen. When you come right down to it, what in hell *can* you do with them?"

"Jesus," he said. "I can show 'em to your wife."

"She'd blush."

"Look—"

"She might even cry," I went on thoughtfully. "Helen cries easily. When she needs a new dress, for example. But she wouldn't get physically aroused, if that's what's on your mind. Nothing gets Helen physically aroused."

He was nonplussed, or unplussed. Or plussed. "Listen," he said. "You got a job, huh?"

"Huh," I said.

"You know what happens when your boss sees these shots?"

"Now that's a different story," I said. "Not at all similar to Helen's case. *He* wouldn't blush."

"Look—"

Look, listen, huh. A spectacular vocabulary. "He wouldn't cry either. He's not exactly the tearful type."

"Listen—"

"Huh," I concluded. "On the other hand, he would get physically aroused. In marked contrast to Helen, he would get very much aroused. He'd probably spend his lunch hour with Jodi, or someone comparable. Or locked in his private bathroom with the pictures."

Al looked uncomfortable. Jodi was still laughing, louder and more happily than ever. I seemed to have fallen upon an advantage, though I wasn't too sure how or why. I stood up, dropped my cigarette onto the rug and squashed it. When you had an advantage, you were supposed to press it. They teach you that on Madison Avenue.

"You said something about a proposition," I said forcefully. "Let's hear it." I almost added *My time is valuable,* but that phrase just then would have been uncomfortably ludicrous.

"Yeah," Al said, slowly. "Yeah, a proposition. I don't know, little man. I think you're all bluff, you know that?"

I didn't answer.

"Then again," he went on, "I don't know if maybe I don't have enough chips to call."

He turned from me to Jodi. "I think this one is a waste of film," he told her. "He don't seem to scare. I could shove him around but that won't do any good. I think we should find somebody else."

"I told you," she cooed. "Harvey's a nice guy."

"That's a matter of opinion," Al said. "I think he just might be a louse. But unless he runs one hell of a bluff, he honestly don't give a damn." He raised both arms to heaven. "Now how in hell," he wanted to know, "can you pressure someone who doesn't give a damn?"

There was a moment of silence. I looked at Jodi, at green knit dress, at crossed legs, at expanse of thigh. I wished Al would go away.

"The proposition," I said.

"Forget it, little man. We'll get somebody else. Go home to your wife."

I shuddered at the very thought. "Let's hear the proposition."

"I told you—"

"Oh, tell him, Al." Jodi smiled. "Harvey's a nice guy."

"Why tell him? What the hell good—"

"I just might go along with it," I said. "Without the pressure. I'm a real oddball."

Looking back on this conversation, the inference is inescapable that I could have sounded like the damnedest dolt on earth. The whole episode, complete with whore and photographs, resembled nothing so much as a blackmail pitch. The "proposition" could only be a demand for money. And here was I, successfully excavated from the pressure, suggesting that I might go along with the proposition for the hell of it. *Just tell me about it,* I was saying in effect, *I'll pay through the nose just to be a good sport.*

But at the time blackmail did not even enter my mind. Perhaps I had watched too many television crime shows—they filled the time between various commercials that I had to catch. Blackmail was too simple. I expected more complicated plotting. At a grand for a half-hour script, one has a right to expect complicated plotting.

Besides, if Jodi was whoring herself into twelve thou a year, money could hardly be their problem. And Jodi was not the blackmailing type. There was something far too honest in her emotional make-up. She wasn't that sneaky.

So I took it for granted that they wanted a patsy, not to pay them, but to perform some task for them. I had no idea what such a task might be. And I was tremendously curious. Chalk it up to the monotony of the day-to-day existence. Chalk it up, if you will, to Hellish Helen who was waiting for me, and who would be so not nice to come home to. Chalk it up to the Vat 69, or to Jodi's creamy thigh. Or to profit and loss.

Al said: "Jodi, I think he's nuts."

"He always was," she said. "A little. But he's a nice guy."

"They finish last."

She looked thoughtful now. I studied her face and her expression was disturbingly familiar. Then it came back to me. She had had just such a look in her pretty eyes when, in bed, she was engaged in figuring out a new way to do it.

"Al," she said, "maybe we ought to tell him."

"Don't be a stupid."

"We should," she said, positive now. "I'm sure of it."

"And if he blabs?"

"He won't, Al. Harvey's a—"

"—nice guy," I put in.

"A nice guy," Jodi said. "Besides, I think he really might go along with it. And he'd be perfect, Al. You know damned well he would be perfect."

The *damned* took me aback. Jodi was not the swearing type.

"I *know* he's perfect," Al was saying now. "That's what I was telling you, and you tried to tell me to leave him out of it. Now I want to leave him out, and *he* wants in, and *you* say he's perfect." He paused a moment to let that sink in. "I think," he wound up, "that *I'm* maybe going nuts."

"Maybe," Jodi said. "But just think about it, Al. He's perfect, just as you said. And if he goes along with it, because he *wants* to, he'll be a lot better than if he's forced into it. When you rape a girl, she doesn't put her heart into it the way she does when she's interested in the game. Right?"

He nodded. The image must have been right up his sewer. I wondered how many girls he had raped, and whether they had put their hearts into it. They evidently had not, because this was the argument which convinced him. He resumed nodding his head, so forcefully that I thought for a moment it might part company with his body, which would have been no major loss. Then he stepped over to me (I was still standing, and smoking a second of Jodi's cigarettes by this time) and jabbed a forceful finger into my chest, as if pushing a doorbell.

"Little man," he said, "I think maybe you've got rocks in your head. But if you want in, you have in. If you don't want it, you will have to for everything which Jodi tells you, because otherwise you could have a bad accident."

"Huh," I said.

"Listen," he said, to both of us. "Look. I am getting out of here, Jodi. This has been a very bad night for me, Jodi. First I take a roll of pictures, which as it turns out we can use for wall paper, or maybe to start a fire in the furnace. Then you and this bird play some kind of Ring Around The Rosie and I don't quite get what is coming off. I am going home, Jodi, and I am going to bed."

"You aren't telling Harvey?"

"You tell him," Al said. "You tell him whatever you want to tell him. And tomorrow you can tell me what the hell is coming off. Okay?"

"Okay," Jodi said.

"Huh," I chimed in.

If you can picture an orangutan stalking off in a huff, you can picture the exit of the Abominable Cameraman. He picked up his sneaky little camera, a pudgy finger smearing the baleful lens, and he hulked haughtily to the door. He opened it, and stepped outside, and the door slammed shut.

That left me alone with Jodi, which was a marked improvement. Jodi paced the floor for a moment or two, and I sat down once again on the couch and time passed on little cat feet. Now and then Jodi turned to me, and cleared her throat, and opened her mouth as if to speak, and closed her mouth, and looked away, and resumed pacing.

"Harvey," she said finally, tired of parading like a caged lion, "I am very sorry."

"Why?"

"That I let Al . . . take pictures. And try to put you on the spot."

"Forget it."

"I'm horribly sorry, Harvey."

"Don't be." I extended a hand plaintively and she put a fresh cigarette between two of my fingers. I let her light it for me. She sank down onto the couch, her rear nestled neatly on top of the long legs that she folded under herself. This pretty process made her dress ride a little higher, so that it was roughly halfway up her thighs and all bunched from hem to waist. She leaned forward, her eyes soulful, and her breasts leaped at me.

"About the proposition—"

"Forget the proposition," I said.

"You mean you're not really interested?"

"I'm interested, Jodi. But let's get to it chronologically. Not too long ago I came floating through your door. You let me in, and I said something inane like *Long time no see,* and then Al slapped me back to the land of the living. Now, something happened in the middle."

She waited for me to say something more. This was awkward, because I was waiting for *her* to say something. Rather lamely I said: "In the middle. What happened?"

"You don't remember?"

"Not a bit of it, woman. Fill me in."

"Why, you silly! We made love, Harvey. What did you think we did, you silly?"

"That's what I thought. It seemed painfully logical. But I don't remember it."

"Well, I do. It was kind of fun."

"Oh," I said.

"It's a shame you don't remember."

"More than a shame," I said, hanging my head. "The memory is half of it. Now it's as if we never did it at all. Of course there are pictures to prove it, but no memories to warm my later years."

"Poor Harvey."

"Did we do anything unusual?"

She wrinkled up her forehead, thinking back. She threw her shoulders back, and this only pushed her breasts out at me a little more dramatically. I let my eyes take a guided tour of her, let myself get mesmerized by the way her perfect body was shaped and molded by the loving hand of a benevolent God. The body was magnificent.

And yet magnificence of form was less than half the story. The sensual appeal of feminine curves cannot be measured in inches or feet, in pounds, shillings or ounces. In her own unpleasant way, my good wife Helen had a body not overwhelmingly dissimilar to Jodi's. The breasts were smaller, but hardly miniscule. The thighs were not so plump, not so well-muscled, but they were by no means bad. There was something else—an aura of excitement, an artistic quality to the twists and turns, the curves and planes. Something that told you at a glance (provided you knew what to look for) that Jodi was a potential source of delight, while Helen could set ice floating in the Caribbean.

"Nothing too unusual," she said, dragging me back to our conversation. "Nothing we hadn't done years ago. In college."

"That doesn't rule much out."

"I know."

"And it was good?"

"Kind of, Harvey. Except you were pretty stoned, weren't you? You didn't exactly know what you were doing. And then I knew Al was there, snapping his silly camera. That took some of the fun out of it. Poor Harvey."

"Poor Jodi," I said.

She uncoiled like a striking serpent, came to her feet and stretched her arms to the skies, or at least to the ceiling. She stood high on the tips of her toes and my eyes were with her every glorious inch of the way. This had been mine once, I remembered. This had brightened college days, this had taught me what my manhood was. And now, because in those long-lost days I had confused success with happiness, Jodi was a whore who loved her work and I was an ad man who hated mine. Now, when I did make love to her, I could not even remember it.

"The proposition," I reminded her.

Slowly she pirouetted, turning her back to me. Slowly her arms descended from the ceiling and she leaned three miles over and touched her toes. I let my eyes focus on her rear. This they did of their own accord.

"The proposition," I managed to say. "With Al."

She straightened up again, slowly, and she turned around, slowly, and her cheeks were roses in bloom, her eyes huge and shining, her lips parted and moist.

"I've got another proposition in mind," she said. "And we can leave Al out of this one."

Her green knit second-skin buttoned down the back. I would have gladly unbuttoned it for her but she did not require my help. Her hands stole behind her back and toyed expertly with buttons. This did more things with her breasts. They leaped across the room at me.

"One button at a time," she said. "There are a lot of buttons. You'll have to be patient, Harvey. You don't look patient at all."

The room was a steam bath. After four years she finished with the buttons. She stepped back, suddenly, and the dress fell off. That's precisely what happened—the dress *fell off.* One moment she was clothed, and the next moment the dress was a green pile upon the carpet, and all that had been under it was my Jodi.

I've mentioned her body, haven't I? Her body of college days, and how perfect that body was, and how the breasts jutted and the waist tucked itself in and the hips flared and the buttocks quivered? How the thighs reached up to the universal V, V for vigor, for vitality, for vim, for voom? I've mentioned all this, haven't I?

I have; I'm sure I have. And I've mentioned, too, how that body had filled out with time, how time did not wither nor custom stale her infinite variety. I had seen the old Jodi nude, and I had seen the new Jodi with clothes on, and now I was seeing the new Jodi nude, a flawless combination of old and new retaining the finest features of each.

She did not walk to me. She flowed to me, her body a symphony of fleshy poetry in motion. She came in like the tide, and her voice was a panther's purr.

"Harvey," she said. "You don't remember the last time, do you?"

"Huh."

"Don't you even move," she said now. "I undressed *you* before. Did *you* know that? And then dressed you again when we were done. Now you just sit there without moving and I'll undress you again, honey."

I sat there, as motionless as possible, and she did just that. Her hands were cold as Dexter's Frozen Dinners. I was not. She took off my shoes and my socks and my slacks and my shirt and my underwear. She ran those soft hands over my body and I reached for her.

"Not here," she breathed. "Not on the couch. The bedroom is right this way. A bed is more comfortable than a couch, don't you think?"

"Sure," I gulped. My mouth was dry. Now why on earth should my mouth be dry?

"This way, Harvey."

Then we were in her bedroom. I could describe her bedroom—the kind of furniture, the type of carpet, the prints on the wall. But why describe her bedroom? It had a bed in it. Enough? More than enough.

"This is my office," she said. And she giggled then, and we were both naked, and I needed her now far more than I needed her years ago. Our arms went around each other, and her big breasts bundled themselves up against my chest.

"Harvey—"

"Jodi—"

Uninspired dialogue at that. My mouth was dry again, and then my mouth was no longer dry because we were kissing and her wet tongue was a long drink. Breasts and belly and thighs, and all there, and all close, and all warm.

As Dempsey hit Firpo, so did we hit the bed. As Cortez explored Mexico, so did we explore each other. I filled my hands with her breasts. I kissed those breasts, and I touched those buttocks, and my hands shouted Open Sesame, and the command was heeded.

Well, it had been a long time. A good many years (or a bad many years) since college and Jodi. A bad many years of Helen, whose hips had sunk a thousand ships. In that length of time a man can forget excellence and accept mediocrity as the normal course of events. Then, if you are very, very fortunate, the spectacular happens upon you.

The spectacular happened upon me—or beneath me, to be more nearly precise. And bombs went off, and choirs sang, and whistles tooted, and Grant took Richmond, and Socrates took poison. I had Jodi's breast for a cushion and Jodi's hips for a safety belt and Jodi's body for a fine and private place. She squirmed and tossed, the ultimate synthesis of genuine passion and the technical virtuosity only a professional can display. She moved and I moved, and she moved and I moved, and she moved, and I moved, and she moved and everything moved—

Slowly the world came back into its own. Slowly the clouds drifted away, the fog lifted, and reality returned. I was lying on my back and Jodi's face hovered above, inches from my own. Her mouth opened.

"There," she whispered. "You won't forget this time, will you?"

I did not have to answer. She turned away from me, her face nestled against her pillow. She fell asleep at once, the healthy sleep of the healthy animal. I lay on my back, my eyes tightly shut, but I did not sleep. I thought instead of Jodi, and I thought of just how far I had come, how I lived now with a streamlined iceberg and peddled monotonous meals and stale cigarettes to Mr. & Mrs. Middle Majority.

It seemed to be my day for reminiscence. There had been Jodi, in the beginning, shortly after God created the heavens and the earth. Then there had been the shoeless time in the bar, and the *Harv, we shouldn't* interlude with Laura Gray. Even then I had been a human being, living a human life. But somewhere, in the course of it all, things changed . . .

As it turned out, it took even longer to get out of the mailroom than it had taken to get into Laura Gray. One year longer, more or less. For the first two months of that year I lived at Laura's humble flat. I dragged my suitcase from the Y and moved in with little ceremony, and Laura and I set sail upon the placid sea of domesticity.

Every morning we awoke together to the farm news, furnished by a nasal-voiced announcer who held sway on her clock-radio. Every morning we turned off the farm news and played hayloft for a spell, after which we showered and brushed our teeth. Then I would shave while she applied makeup, and then she cooked either bacon and eggs or ham and eggs, each an equally valid rebellion against her ancestry. And then off to work went we, she to the secretarial pool and I to the mailroom. Then home came we, sweat-stained and weary, grabbing dinner at a luncheonette around the corner from our 69th Street home, and killing time one way or another until it was a respectable hour for mattress machinations.

A scant two months, and then our mad and passionate affair withered and turned to dust. There were a great many reasons. On the purely physical side, I think another month of Laura would have killed me. She liked to bite, and to scratch, and to dig with her claws and to hit—in fact, I finally took to calling her *Justine.* This was before Lawrence Durrell, I was thinking of De Sade. The scratches and bites didn't embarrass me too much—I probably wore them with an air of callow triumph—but the pain, in time, grew unbearable.

Then there was our different position in the lists of commerce. She was a secretary while I was a mail clerk, and this fact remained no matter who was on top during the night. Account executives made passes at her, and copywriters made passes at her, and once in a while a partner of the firm cast a sidelong look at her. And here she was, shacking up with a clod from the mailroom, for the love of God.

Besides, domesticity paled. I was too young for it. The delight of having a sure conquest at home failed eventually to compensate for the moral obligation to refrain from making a fresh conquest. Our affair ran its course and died and despite mutual tears at parting, I am sure we were both equally delighted to be on the loose again.

This time the Y didn't snare me. It was autumn. I went downtown and shared a one-room apartment with four hundred and thirty-seven cockroaches, a fourth-floor walk up on Barrow Street in the heart of Greenwich Village. It should have been romantic—I was young enough to appreciate that sort of thing. Somehow, it was only verminous.

And so I toiled, and toiled. The months went by and the seasons changed, and I remained in the mailroom, carting correspondence from desk to free-form desk and waiting patiently for a promotion. There were five of us in the mailroom, all hungry to break into the ad game, and all of us united by one other common bond.

We were never promoted.

No one, it seemed, was promoted. Periodically one of us was fired, and periodically one of us quit, and the agency quickly replaced the departed one with still another young hopeful. I decided that Tom Stanton, S sub-two, was the most hilarious practical joker since Guy Fawkes. I was doomed to a lifetime in the mailroom, a lifetime of $40-a-week minus deductions.

Then came August. And somewhere, I suppose, someone died, because a man named John Fehringer came up to me, tapped me on the shoulder, and said *See you a min, keed.*

I translated this mentally—I had learned, in my year with MGSR&S branch of the post office, how to translate Newspeak into English automatically. I went off with Fehringer, and he gave me a filtered cigarette and a filtered smile, in that order. I accepted both.

"I hear good things about you," he said. "The word from up high has it that you should be given room to grow. Like to try a stint of copywriting, Harv Boy?"

"Well," I said, "sure."

He took me to another huge room, into which I had occasionally delivered pieces of copy and mysterious manila envelopes. He showed me a desk and told me that it was going to be my desk. It was old and wobbly, the kind they sell for ten dollars, but, by God, it was all mine. There were drawers in it, and I could fill those drawers with my things. There was a top on that desk, and when no one was looking I could put my feet on it. It was my desk, my first desk, and I shelved it in my mind next to my first love affair.

Fehringer brought me some artwork for a magazine ad, with the key copy penciled in and with catchwords scrawled on a batch of file cards. "This is the ad," he said. "Like?"

The artwork showed a half-naked girl drawing the string on a sixty-pound bow. It was an advertisement for Bull's-Eye Spaghetti.

"Like," I said.

"In here," he said, pointing at the white space at the bottom of the layout, "is where we tell them that if they buy this cruddy spaghetti they can grow boobs like the broad in the picture. Or whatever we're telling 'em this week. It's all on the file cards. You turn it into English and put it in there."

"I see," I said.

"It's a pipe," he told me. "Easy-do does it, Harv Boy. If it sails smoothly you can keep this desk."

"And if it doesn't?"

"Then you're fired," he said sweetly. "Have fun, keed. Just take your time and hurry. Run it up the flagpole and see who salutes."

He left. I sat in my desk for a minute, getting the feel of it, and then I started to turn Bull's-Eye Spaghetti into English. It was a pipe, and easy-do did it. I got a head-swelling collection of compliments from the goof I turned the gunk over to, and I celebrated that night by picking up a Bohemian girl in Greenwich Village.

Her name was Saundra. She had long black hair and purple eye shadow, and she was not quite as bad as she sounds. Or maybe she was. She seemed all right at the time. I found her over a cup of cappuccino in something called Le Cul de Sac, where she was telling a group of bearded young men just how horrible Madison Avenue was. It was amusing, because I was certain she got nosebleeds every time she went north of Fourteenth Street. But I kept a straight face.

"You have some interesting ideas," I butted in, "but I don't think you have a straight line on the ad game. It's a little more complex than all that."

"Oh?" She favored me with a look. "Are you in advertising?"

"I handle the Bull's-Eye Spaghetti account over at MGSR&S." It was a more-than-slight exaggeration, but I could have told her I was a Third Assistant Skyhook at TWA&T. She was duly impressed.

"I've had too much coffee," I said. "Let's get a drink."

We got a drink. She was terribly young, and terribly naive, and, when you came right down to it, stupid as the whole Jukes family. I cried on her shoulder about the Ulcer Gulch rat race, told her how I ached to get away from it and write the Great

American Novel in a humble garret. Midway through the fourth drink she was deciding to be my constant inspiration in the wars against crass commercialism. Midway through the fifth drink I had my hand in her leotards. We had the sixth drink in my Barrow Street roach farm, where she took off all her clothes so that she wouldn't feel inhibited.

As it turned out, she did not feel inhibited, not in the least. She was thin, with cute if bite-sized breasts. I could have counted her ribs, if I had been so inclined. A lean horse for a long ride, say the Arabs knowingly, and Saundra proved them right.

I snacked on her little bite-sized breasts while she warbled about the meeting of true minds. I dined on her body with hungry hands while she told me how I was selling my soul to the devil of commerce.

Then I ran her up the flagpole, and everybody saluted . . .

There my reverie gave way to sleep. I'd sort of planned on thinking back to the beginning with Helen, but sleep saved me from such heartache, and I forgot all about Helen and dreamed pleasant dreams of Jodi. The night passed slowly in slumber, and then dawn winked too bright an eye at me, and Jodi was beaming at me.

A wonderful girl, Jodi. She cooked breakfast and fed it to me without saying a word, and I for my part said nothing at all. I finished my third cup of coffee, thinking all the while of a suitable explanation to heave at Helen, and then, finally, I said: "Good morning, Jodi."

"Good morning," she said. "Did you forget?"

"Forget what?"

"Last night."

"Jodi," I said, "I shall sooner forget my name."

"You're nice, Harvey."

I lit the ends of a pair of cigarettes and passed one to her. Then I remembered in part why I was still at Jodi's, instead of being on the 8:12 out of Rockland County.

"Jodi," I said, "the proposition."

She nodded sagely. "Listen to this, Harvey," she said. "You may like it."

CHAPTER 5

There was time, in my not particularly innocent youth, when I considered myself an essentially moral type, a young man who was a bit shrewd perhaps, something of a corner-cutter and a doubt-benefiter, but nevertheless containing a solidly moral and ethical core.

We all believe that when young, I suppose. Some men—I imagine they should be considered the lucky ones—never do find out the truth. Alas, those self-ignorant ones are not to be found in the advertising profession, not outside the mailroom at any rate. It was relatively early in the game that I discovered what was really at the core of me—a black, sinful, unashamed and overwhelming concern, interest and fascination for number one. Or, I should say, Number One. Me. I quite frankly don't know what I'd do without me.

"You may like it," said Jodi, and I'd never realized till then just how well she really knew me. Her proposition, if it included someone like Al the Neanderthalus Chicagus, would inevitably be something highly illegal. Only a man who has learned to live with his nasty true self can be expected to sit still when someone begins a criminal or sinful proposition with the words, "You may like it."

She expected me to sit still. Ergo, and all that.

I gained my precious self-understanding, by the by, at just around the same time as I was promoted from the ten-dollar desk and the Bull's-Eye Spaghetti account, as so often happens in real life or whatever it is I've been doing for the past thirty-one years. The promotion and the self-understanding both were the end result of a little conversation I had with Fehringer one day after I'd been hitting the bull's-eye for about seven months.

I looked up from my pencil that day, and saw Furry Fehringer approaching my desk. He wore one of those smiles that makes you instinctively look to see if there's a knife in his hand.

As a matter of fact, there was. But not for me.

"Min, keed," he said. I think his years in the racket had made him learn to hate the English language, and he was gradually trying to divorce himself from it completely. He was doing a pretty good job.

"Sure thing," I said. Both sensible English words, pronounced the way schoolteachers do it in Iowa, which just goes to show how new I was.

"Around the quad," he said. "Kay?"

"Kay." I was learning.

I got to my feet, and we roamed together around the quad. That is, we traversed the corridors of MGRS&S, up one pastel alleyway and down another, every once in a while passing that section of translucent glass-brick wall with the eight-foot free-form pink beer bottle in it celebrating a five-year-old MGRS&S coup, and Fehringer newspoke about this and that, mostly conversational chaff, from which I herewith extract the wheat, with my responses:

"You know Tom Stanton, eh, keed?"

"Uh huh."

"Brought you into the corps, didn't he?"

"Uh huh." (My responses gained in directness what they may have lacked in vivacity.)

"Feeling of loyalty, eh?"

(Dangerous ground, that. I wasn't *that* new. Was Fehringer a loyal Stanton man, or was his suzerain in our hierarchy? The best answer, I decided, was no answer at all.) "Well," I said, "you know how it is."

"Mmm. Just traded the flivver in, did I tell you?"

"Oh?"

"Mmm. Trade in every two years. Like to keep the old boat, sentimental attachment and all, but got to be practical. New one cuts the mustard. Sense?"

I nodded. "Sense," I said.

"Pity about Tom," he said.

I endeavored to look as blank as I felt. "Pity?"

"Booze. Fifteen to one in the club car lab now, you know. Poured into Westport every night."

"I didn't know that."

"Been covering for him, holding the flanks. Loyalty myself, you know. Sentimental attachment. Grand guy."

"Sure."

"Pity," he said again, and gloomed at the pink beer bottle on the way by. "Used to cut the mustard."

"Uh huh."

"Got to look out for myself," he said. "Wife and kiddies, that bit. Name and game, you know. Expect a hassle on the Wilmot Toothpaste. Sales on the downydoo."

"Oh?"

"Like to have you in my corner, Harv. Step up, eh? Think it over."

And we went back to our respective desks.

I thought it over. Fehringer claimed he'd been doing Tom Stanton's work for a while now. He had the game, and he wanted the name. All I had to do was manufacture a little damaging evidence concerning Bull's-Eye Spaghetti—which was also, ultimately, in Tom Stanton's bailiwick—and I could have a piece of the game for myself. When Fehringer moved up, so would I.

I thought it over. All afternoon at the desk I thought it over, and homeward bound on the IRT I thought it over some more.

Come to think of it, I wonder just how many decisions to foreswear goodness and virtue in favor of evil and degradation were made homeward bound on the rush-hour trains of the IRT, between Lexington–51st and the depths of the Village. (For the benefit of foreign citizens the IRT is the Metro. Geh?) This daily voyage involves three trains and a lot of subterranean walking, all in the close company of a surly mob which, for pure meanness of spirit and nastiness of behavior, holds no equal in all history with the possible exception of Robespierre's crowd in the French Revolution. (Could it be that old Tom Jefferson's—what a copywriter!—second revolution never came about simply because, for the urban masses, all revolutionary humors are dissipated in the mere process of getting to and from work? A thought I toss out for political scientists in the arena.)

At any rate, I thought Friend Fehringer's proposition over all afternoon at my desk, and couldn't see myself being such a dastard as he proposed, not for anything in the world. How could I possibly look myself in the eye ever again, having betrayed a kindness in such a manner? For it was, truly, Tom Stanton S sub-two who had given me my start in this rewarding (sic) profession.

On the Lex local, strap-hanging, between 51st Street and Grand Central, I thought it over some more. And subtly, without my really noticing it at all, my thinking began its insidious change. My thoughts were still in opposition to Fehringer the Ferret, but my reasoning had metamorphosed. Now, I was thinking: What if Fehringer doesn't get away with it? After all, Tom Stanton is S sub-two, no easy man to diddle. Wouldn't my smart move be to avoid the issue entirely? Thus remaining both morally pure and occupationally safe.

Walking underground from the Lex local to the 42nd Street shuttle, my busy brain turned to contemplation of the Bull's-Eye Spaghetti account. Was that an occupation, after all, worthy of safeguarding?

Wedged amid the snarling weasels on the cross-town shuttle from Grand Central to Times Square, I thought about Fehringer's job. I might, could possibly have that job myself, if Fehringer bootstrapped (or bootlicked, or booted) himself upward. With its increments, ah, yes. One could taxi homeward, lollygagging in blissful solitude in acres of back seat, whilst the taxi driver did all the sweating and snarling in one's stead.

Traversing the tile-walled corridors from shuttle to 7th Avenue Express, and riding that Profane Comedy southward, I began to see the justice of Fehringer's proposal. He was absolutely right actually. Tom Stanton *was* a rather heavy boozer. He'd been glowing rather brightly, in fact, when he'd met and hired me. Feral Fehringer was undoubtedly accurate in his claim that he had been carrying the ball for Tom Stanton lo these many moons. Name and game, indeed and exactly. A ball carrier in need is a ball carrier indeed. And I was surely worthy of promotion myself. Hadn't my earnest efforts on behalf of Italian clotheslines been met with universal and unequivocal approval among the higher-ups?

By the time I made the change at 14th Street from the express to the local, I had made another change as well, and somewhat more significant. What, I was currently asking myself, had Tom Stanton really done for me after all? Hired me to the mailroom, that was what, something any personnel manager or employment agency in the business could have done just as well. And what had Furtive Fehringer done for me? He'd rescued me from the mailroom and started my upward climb via Bull's-Eye Spaghetti, for number one. And he'd offered me a helping hand to climb yet another rung of the ladder of excess. Fehringer the bell ringer. Put your money on Fraternal Fehringer, the pupil's choice.

But still, you know, some tattered remnant of my earlier self-respect still clung to my hunched shoulders. Rationalizations were all well and good, but something more was needed.

I was still living with Saundra at that time, and so I broached the subject to her that evening. I felt the need for a confidante, for someone to assure me that my choice was right and proper and good and beneficial, and that I could get away with it.

Saundra seemed, at the time, like the logical choice. She hated Madison Avenue so. Our nocturnal exertions were punctuated by manifestoes, our foreplay was fortified by foreign-born philosophies, our sex was ever seasoned with sociology.

According to Saundra, the capitalist society was a jungle, of the most primitive kind. For the individual in such a jungle, there were three choices open, three avenues of life: First, one could choose to be a timid tiny creature, with a burrow in which one hid from the ferociousness outside. Wage slaves and other roamers of the rutted routine were such stuff as timid tiny creatures were made on. Second, one could choose to be a lion or a panther, stalking the jungle, tearing from its richness whatever one could get. Financiers and Wall Street and Madison Avenue were panthers. Third, one could choose to be an eagle, and get the hell out of the jungle completely, by soaring above it all, swooping down into it only rarely for sustenance and otherwise wafting among the clods, thinking higher thoughts. Saundra and her unwashed friends were, if you could believe it, eagles.

According to Saundra, timid tiny creatures deserved everything they got, and in all justice were fit prey for panther and eagle alike. Panthers, on the other hand, were contemptible for their lack of intellectualism or morality, but were worthy of respect for their graceful ferocity. Eagles, of course, were the chosen few.

Saundra, I think, was never quite sure exactly what yours truly was. I lived more or less like a timid creature, but I had moments of aspiration toward pantherdom, and I seemed somehow able to converse with eagles on their own air.

In essence, therefore, I believed it reasonably safe to inform Saundra of my decision to join the ranks of panthers with one mighty bound upon the back of Tom Stanton. Her contempt for Stanton—for all advertising men who compounded their original sin by living in a commuter suburb—seemed to be sufficient to keep her away from any pity for the man. And her grudging respect for panthers should keep her at my side after the announcement was made.

I arrived at our den of iniquity—the term 'pad' was not at that time as yet hip, nor was the term 'hip'—exhausted not from my labors but from my homewending, and over platters of Dinty Moore beef stew I told her of Philistine Fehringer's proposition, and of my own decisions thereunto.

Alas, it only goes to show that one never knows women! At least not emancipated Bohemian women who have left the middle class behind but haven't yet decided whether that makes them upper class or lower class. Saundra's reaction to my disclosure was as violent as it was unexpected.

"Harvey, you don't mean it? You'd—you'd stick a knife in the back of the man who befriended you? Who got you your *job?*"

"Well," I said, "he *is* a lush."

"That only proves," she snapped back, "that he has a conscience. I wouldn't be surprised if he had a very delicate soul. Look at the way you two met. He came to you instantly because you didn't have any shoes on."

"So did the waiter," I said.

"Don't try to be funny, Harvey," she said commandingly. "I think that's a terrible thing. If I thought for one minute that the man to whose bosom I had—"

"And a lovely bosom it is," I said.

"Don't try to change the subject. Mr. Stanton was very good to you. How you could even think of—"

She went on and on that way. I had forgotten one important truth: Early upbringing remains behind, no matter how many logical or emotional overlays are laminated on it. And had I ever mentioned that Saundra hailed originally from Doughboy, Nebraska? (If you don't believe that such a place exists, friend, you just look it up in that miserable encyclopedia that smooth-talking door-to-door son-of-a-bitch sold you last year.) Way down beneath all the eagles and panthers and timid tiny creatures, Doughboy, Nebraska still burned in the heart of my raven-stressed Saundra. It was Doughboy that was talking now, not pinko sociology professors from Czechoslovakia. And Doughboy, it seemed, was just as long-winded as that other Saundra I had come to know and love so well.

And all at once I realized she was right, though for the wrong reason. Of *course* I should remain loyal to Tom Stanton! My evil little brain went clickety-click, and the whole frabjous plot lay nekkid before me. *Alors!*

I leaped up from the table. I never did care much for beef stew anyway. Rushing around to Saundra's side, I embraced her, crying, "You're right! You've made me see the light, Saundra, and tomorrow morning I will go straight to Tom Stanton and warn him of Fehringer's evil scheme."

She studied me suspiciously. "Do you mean that?"

"Cross my heart," I said, crossing my heart.

"Because if you don't," she said, "I certainly wouldn't want to have anything to do with—"

She was far from finished, of course. She intended to talk all night, no matter how often I agreed with her. So I pinched her left nipple and said, "Darling, speak to me only with thine eyes." That was a little euphemistic cue-phrase we'd developed for a certain amorous variant of which I had become quite a devotee of late, since it prohibited speech on Saundra's part.

"You haven't finished supper," she said.

"It isn't beef stew I want to eat," I said gallantly. My future had suddenly opened before me, rosy and soft, elating me in all sorts of ways. As the cave-man returned from a successful hunt or joust, full of his triumph, and could find no better capper for the whole thing than to throw his mate onto the floor of the cave and prod her with his maledom a while, so I.

I grabbed my Saundra's little breasts—as hard as young rocks, but much more delicious—and led her by them to the bedroom. By the time we passed the threshold, she was giggling and her little tail was wagging just fine. Bohemian ranter or Doughboy doughgirl, both of those were finally incidental. Saundra was, elementally, a sex machine. She had two buttons in front, and both were marked ON.

I'm a lazy man, all in all, and Saundra loved to pander to my laziness. Our conjunction now took its usual—but far from routine—course. Fully clothed, I reclined upon our wrinkled bed, still musky from this morning's pre-breakfast calisthenics. Saundra, narrow body and all awiggle, pink tongue-tip trembling between her lips, proceeded to undress me while thus I lay in regal lassitude. My shoes and socks she removed, then nibbled my toes a while and tickled my soles. Pulling off her sweater and bra, she next knelt at the foot of the bed and carefully placed my feet. Right foot to left breast, the hard dark burning nipple between first and second toes, likewise left foot to right breast, and then I wiggled my toes for her benefit, while she giggled and wiggled and squealed. A silly thing, but we both enjoyed it.

Then, her eyes now gleaming bright, she would push my feet away and come climbing up over me, to sit astride my waist and unbutton my shirt while I unzipped her dungarees. Man's dungarees, thank God. The female variety has the fly on the side, designed no doubt by some anti-social type or a believer in the theories of Malthus.

In order to remove my shirt, she would have to lean close over me, while I propped up a bit on my elbows. This position was perfect for windshield wiper: Left breast, kiss, right breast, kiss, left breast, kiss, and so on. The T-shirt involved a bit more work, but was worth it.

At this juncture, Saundra liked to lie prone upon me a moment or two, and nibble on my chest. I always took this opportunity to push her dungarees and panties down over her hips and halfway down her thighs, which was as far as I could reach in that position. I then liked to treat her buttocks like a drum, slapping little stinging syncopated rhythms on them, while she squirmed in delight beneath my hands.

When we'd worked this routine as far as we could stand, Saundra would next writhe off me and, standing beside the bed, finish removing her dungarees and panties. Then she would stand close enough for me to do some in-fighting while she wrestled with my belt, and stripped away the last two pieces of my clothing.

Then she spoke to me, for a while, only with her eyes. For very good and obvious reasons.

There were times when I preferred to simply lie in state during this interlude, passively appreciating her attentions upon me. But there were other times, and this was one of them, when I was in high spirits and wanted to reciprocate in kind, a treat that Saundra found absolutely delightful. She was, as I have said, a lean and bony thing, all flesh and bone, but with wiry muscles and unquenchable energies. She found it impossible to remain still whenever I so much as touched her. Her shoulders twitched, waggling her bite-size breasts, her hips gyrated, her legs trembled, her arms waved around, and she was generally and delightfully in motion. This motion increased tenfold when I chose to perform upon her the equivalent of her service for me. The dear hard nipples of her lovely breasts would scrape upon my belly, her head would nod in staccato agreement, her hips would pulse madly upon me as I once more slapped the small globes of her buttocks, her knees would beat upon the bed beyond my ears, and her hands would caress in fine imitation of my own handiwork upon her.

Yet she was always the one who first ended this preliminary bout, coming up gasping for air, her face bright with sweat, her mouth lax and passion-drugged. "Now," she would whisper, unable to talk aloud. "Oh, now, Harvey, do it to me now, take me, do it!"

And I would slap her ringingly, here and there, which only made her desire more intense, and she would squirm around, sitting now in position similar to the one she'd taken when unbuttoning my shirt, though now with a significant difference, and thus she would sit, writhing and pulsing, the muscles working beneath the skin of her flat stomach, her breasts bouncing with her exertions, her head flung back, eyes squeezed shut and mouth hanging open, her hands prodding me like a lifeguard performing artificial respiration. And I, lazy and comfortable and effete male, would lie in pleasant bliss upon my back, a silly smile upon my face, a passive but interested observer as Saundra agitated over me, working herself to a climax.

What a wonder that girl was! Undoubtedly stupid, as I have earlier said, and full of all sorts of philosophical eyewash, Bohemianism interwoven with Doughboyism, but Lord love a duck was she good in bed! And making love was such a natural and basic thing to her that she crested more readily and more often than any other girl I have ever known, before or since.

So we would continue, until she would suddenly go rigid, arms twisted upward and fingers curled, mouth wide-stretched in a silent scream, and my hands would rub her, finding every muscle taut and tense, her nipples fairly tingling beneath my touch, her abdomen as hard as a wall.

Thus she would climb to the peak before I, but she was good about it. She always rushed back down the mountain to join me again, so that now we could climb together.

And for our second stage, our positions would be more or less reversed. She would be tired now, worn from her labors, and I chivalrously would allow her to take my place. In legend, men have owed their strength to the length of their hair or the whim of some deity or some other such unlikely source. My own strength would arise much more directly. Saundra's first exertions never failed to inspire me, and I believe that I have never risen to the occasion with any other woman as strongly or as well as with Saundra.

Ah, if only she hadn't been such an utter bean-brain! I might have never become involved with Helen. And who knows, then, what my future might have been. Surely not Jodi and her illegal proposition.

At any rate, the day that I decided to remain true to Tom Stanton turned out to be one of the best encounters that Saundra and I ever had together. And the next day, refreshed in body and mind, I waited till I saw an important client enter Fetid Fehringer's office—so I was certain he would be in there for a while, and wouldn't see me leave my desk nor know my destination—and then I went up to talk to Tom Stanton.

It was one of the very few times I'd seen the man since he'd hired me. Looking at him now, I saw the increased puffiness of face, laxity of expression, since that day so many months before when I sat unshod in the bar. Fehringer undoubtedly was right; Tom Stanton was drinking himself out of efficiency.

But this was no time for soulless calculation. This was a time for loyalty. And I was full of loyalty, stoked to the gunwales with loyalty, fairly reeking with loyalty.

Once I got past Tom's receptionist—a nice bit that, and available from what I'd heard around the water cooler—and saw Tom himself, I got directly to the meat of the problem.

"Tom," I said, using his first name for the first time, "you're the man who brought me into MGSR&S in the first place and I want you to know that I'm grateful."

"That's good," he said. A faint aroma of bourbon was in the air.

"And so," I continued, "when I heard of something in the wind that could be dangerous to you, I knew at once what my duty was."

He became a bit more alert. "Dangerous? To me?"

"Your boy Fehringer came to see me yesterday," I said, and went on from there, outlining everything that Fehringer had said and everything that Fehringer had implied.

When I was finished my tale of deception and intrigue, a dejected and beaten man slumped in his easy-foam chair before me.

"He's right, Harv," said Tom Stanton. "I've been slipping lately. I've left myself wide open for a back-stabbing like this. Old Fehringer! I might have known."

"I thought I'd let you know at once," I said, "so you'd have time to plan your counterattack."

"Counterattack," he echoed hopelessly. "What can I do? The man's an intriguer, he's been planning this for months. Old Fehringer! Got the knife out for me, and nothing I can do."

"Ah, but there is," I said. "Tom, I'm loyal to you, you know that. I want to help."

He looked up at me, hope springing into his eyes. "Is there something cooking in your double-boiler, Harv, boy?" he asked me.

"There sure is, Tom. Fehringer's going to play the eager-beaver a while now, till he's ready to spring the double whammo. All you have to do is let him swipe a project, and let the big men see him at it."

"Bad tactics, Harv," he said, shaking his head. "Right away, they'll know old Tom is slipping."

"For the nonce, Tom, for the nonce. But catch this: You work up a presentation anyway, you see? Meanwhile. I'm in Fehringer's bailiwick, and I sabotagerooney *his* little effort, and at the next conference *splat!*"

He sat up, the light of battle dawning in his eyes. "You'll do that for me, Harv, boy?"

"I'm loyal, Tom," I said simply.

Now there was a thing that year called the sailor hat, only for girls not for boys. At a conference, Tom allowed Fehringer to grab the project away from him, and said only one sentence to

Fehringer, which would ring in the big boy's minds a few weeks later: "I'll be glad to have you take a stab at this, boy; I want to know if you're ready for the big time."

And Fehringer, poor Fehringer, smiled his little smile and said, "I think I'm ready, Tom."

Six weeks later, I had Fehringer's job, and the sailor hat account was using Tom Stanton's presentation. *Don't say no till you've seen the proposition from every side.* No one told me that, I thought of it all by myself. If you're going to be immoral, you really ought to be smart about it.

Which was why I replied to Jodi, "Yes, I may like it. Let's hear it."

"It's a one-shot proposition, Harv," she said. "There may be repeat jobs, but I'm not sure of that. Here's the story: There's a man in Brazil right now, and he wants something that happens to be in New York right now. This thing can't just be sent to him, because the federal government would grab it, and there'd be a lot of trouble all around. So it has to be smuggled out of the United States and smuggled into Brazil."

"But surely," I said, "there are regular smuggling routes already. For dope, say, or gold."

"There's very little smuggling going *out* of the country," she said. "Besides, this is too dangerous to be trusted to the regular systems. What the boys have been looking for is an honest Joe, a guy with no record and no file, and a guy rich enough to take a trip to Brazil anyway. He can carry the stuff, and nobody the wiser."

"And?"

She smiled. "You want to know what's in it for you. Five thousand dollars, and a two-week all-expense-paid trip to Brazil. With me."

"With you?"

"A man traveling with his wife," she said sweetly, "is less suspect than any other kind of man."

"And what is this cargo I'm supposed to deliver?"

She shook her head. "I don't know. Except it's valuable." She lit a new cigarette. "Well, Harv? Are you interested?"

I suddenly remembered the slogan in Fehringer's sailor hat presentation and I burst into laughter. "Spend your summer under a great big sailor," I said. "That means yes."

CHAPTER 6

Haste makes waste. Look before you leap. Rome was not built in a day. The mills of the Gods grind slow but they grind exceeding small.

I quote the above, not to demonstrate my familiarity with banality down through the ages, but to point out just how thoroughly our platitudes have lost touch with the era in which we live. Tell the twentieth century male that haste makes waste and he'll reply—quickly—that ours is an economy of waste and he's merely being economical. Look before you leap, friend, and the door will be shut before you're through it. And, while Rome may not have been *built* in a day, it was certainly *sacked* in a day. As for the mills of the Gods . . . well, forget about them.

Which is all just a lap-dissolve into the message of the moment. Jodi and I leaped quickly, without wasting time looking around. We leaped furiously. There was no time to play games.

In the first place, the cargo, whatever it might be, had to be in Brazil in a hurry. This man in Brazil (and here I pictured a fat Sidney Greenstreet type with a tropical suit and overactive perspiration glands) was impatient. He needed this cargo. And, while I had a mental image of this Man In Brazil, I had no image whatsoever of the cargo. But he needed it, by Allah's beard, and he needed it with bells on.

In the second place, this was smuggling, and smuggling was illegal. Now neither Jodi nor I were traditional law-abiders, but smuggling in the eyes of the federal government is somewhat more serious an offense than either prostitution (Jodi's crime) or false advertising (mine, repeatedly). Both Jodi and I, though more than willing to do the deed, echoed Macbeth in hoping that if it were done, would it were done quickly. The sooner we were in Brazil, and the sooner the cargo was delivered, and the sooner we were *back* from Brazil, the sooner we would be safe, again.

"Passports," Jodi said. "I think you have to have a passport to go to Brazil, Harvey. Or to get back from Brazil. I forget which."

"Either way," I said, "we need them."

"How long does it take to get a passport?"

"Months," I said hollowly. "Many months. Red tape, and all."

For five or ten minutes we sat in Jodi's apartment and thought about the many months we would have to wait before we could get our passports. For five or ten minutes we sat, chewing our tongues, and preparing to cry. And then, casually, I said: "Of course, I already have a passport."

"You do?"

"Mmmmm," I said. "I took Helen to Europe a year ago. We went and looked at all the things you're supposed to look at, and I met a Pigalle whore while she went shopping for shoes."

"Is yours still good, Harvey?"

"Sure," I said.

"Why, you silly! Then we don't have anything to worry about."

"We don't?"

"I have a passport," she said. "I have a perfectly fine passport, because six months ago there was this gentleman who was going to Europe, and he wanted me to—"

She broke off, snapping the poor sentence right in the middle. Jodi, alas, was somewhat embarrassed to talk about her professional career in front of me. This embarrassment was something relatively new, since she'd been delighted to discuss the theory and practice of whoring the day we renewed our happy acquaintance. And, strangely, the same reserve was developing within me; I was unwilling to discuss my profession, a subtler sort of whoring, now that Jodi and I were fleshmates once more.

"Wait," I said. "We're supposed to be husband and wife."

"That's right."

"But we aren't," I said. "Your passport is in your name, and mine is in my name, and we're not married. So how on earth can we travel as husband and wife?"

She poured me a fresh cup of coffee, passed the Vat 69 bottle to me, and pointed from the Scotch to the coffee. I took the hint and sweetened my Brazilian brew.

"Harvey," she said, sounding a little like a melodious version of Al, "don't be a stupid."

I looked at my watch. It was getting to be eleven o'clock, and around that time even a casual sort of person is expected to report to MGSR&S and get to work running somebody up some flagpole or other. I took a sip of the alcoholic coffee and squinted at her over the brim of the cup.

"A stupid?"

"A very stupid," she said. "You have a passport and I have a passport. And all we need to travel as man and wife is a marriage license."

"A marriage license?"

"Of course. Then everyone will realize we got married *after* we got the passports. Which is perfectly valid, and which leaves the passports every bit as valid."

Now she was beginning to make sense. I may or may not have been a stupid, but I could see the merit in what she was saying. Still, I had to get to the office. So all I had to do was hurry on to MGSR&S, while she went out and picked us up a marriage license—Wait.

"Jodi," I said. "Really, girl, that's all well and good, but you don't understand. I mean, girl, how can we come by a little thing like a marriage license?"

"Easy."

"Have it forged?" I asked brightly. "I suppose Anthropoid Al knows someone who's handy with a pen but—"

"Not a forged one, Harvey. A real one."

"So much the better," quothe I. "Very much the better. But how and where does one acquire a real marriage license?"

"I'm not sure where," she said. "Anyplace, I guess. But the how part is easy, Harvey."

I watched while she carefully broke a seeded roll in two, spread butter upon each half in turn, and stuffed bites down her throat. When the roll was gone I was still patiently waiting.

She said: "It's simple, Harvey. We get married."

•   •   •

So I never did get to the office that day. Instead, I got married.

First, of course, I explained to Jodi that I already *was* married, for better or for worse, as they say in ceremonies. And while divorcing Helen may have been an admirable notion, it was an unwieldy solution. It would take even longer than arranging for fresh passports.

"You really ought to divorce Helen," Jodi told me, her eyes calm and serious. "I mean afterward, when we get back from Brazil. Not now, but later on."

"Jodi—"

"I know what you're going to tell me," she said. "You are already married. I know that, Harvey. And you know it, and maybe even your wife knows it, though from what you said about her it's hard to tell. But somewhere in Maryland there's a little guy behind a marriage license counter, and *he* doesn't know you're married."

"That," I said, "is bigamy."

"So," she said, "what?"

So what indeed. I went, not to my office, but to the garage wherein I had deposited my ranch wagon the night before. Just a night ago, a night that seemed like ages. I took the car back, power-steered to Jodi's hotel, power-braked at the curb, and went in for her. She came out with two suitcases. We were taking virtually nothing, but one suitcase, she insisted, would make a bad impression upon the Justice of the Peace. So we took two empty ones instead of a single full one, and we loaded them into the rear end of the wagon, and we loaded ourselves into the front end of the wagon, and I pointed the wagon at Maryland's marriage mill, and we set out.

The town for which we were bound was providentially named Cherry Park, for obvious reasons. It was on Maryland's northern border, and it was the marriage capital of the area, since neither a blood test nor a waiting period was required there. This made it a paradise for impulsive souls and syphilitics, and Jodi and I qualified on the first count if not the second. Huzzah for Cherry Park, where all roads lead to City Hall, and where an astounding number of young things park their cherries every day!

Huzzah, indeed.

We went to City Hall, found the marriage license bureau (which was not hard, since it dominated two rooms of the three-room city hall), and filled out brief forms. We walked next door, where there was a line at the Justice of the Peace's little shanty. Finally it was our turn. She said she did, and I said I did, and he said we could. I gave the license, signed and duly noted in Maryland's ledgers, to Jodi, who folded it neatly and placed it in her purse. And back we climbed into the ranch wagon.

"Now what?" I wondered aloud. "Back to New York?"

"No," she said.

"No?"

"No." She let out a long breath. "I've never been married before," she said. "And I have never before had a wedding night, and I would feel rotten spending my wedding night in my own apartment. Find a good motel, Harvey. And then we'll have a good wedding night."

It was not hard locating a motel. The motel industry is a natural in a marriage mill, and the enterprising fellows of Cherry Park were missing no bets. We found a place called Honeymooner Lodge, and I parked the wagon and carried our two suitcases out of it. They were part of a set of matched luggage, which should have shattered the we-never-did-this-before illusion, but this hardly mattered. I walked to the desk and signed the book Mr. and Mrs. Harvey Christopher and only felt like half a liar. The son behind the desk didn't even ask to see our license, and I could have killed him. I mean, we had a license, and I wished he would ask for it.

Our room was clean and spacious. It had a huge double bed, and almost before I had closed the door Jodi was leaping happily upon the bed, bouncing hither and yon to test the springs.

"I'll bet you're starved," I said. "I mean, nothing to eat since breakfast, and that was long ago. We ought to be able to find a decent restaurant down the road, and—"

"We will," she said. "After."

"After?"

"After," she said positively. She was wearing a black dress (inappropriate as hell; whoever heard of getting married in a black dress?) and she proceeded to correct the inappropriateness of the garment by the simple expedient of removing it. The girl had not only gotten married without an unblack dress, but beneath it she wore a black bra. Lacy, and peekaboo in style, and provocative. Then she took it off, and her big boobs beamed at me, and I stopped thinking about bras and dresses and began thinking very seriously about Jodi.

"We have to consummate our marriage," she said, her eyes a-twinkle. "If we don't, you could get an annulment. I don't want you to get an annulment, Harvey."

"But our marriage is bigamous to begin with."

"Still," she said, "I don't want us to get an annulment. So let's make sure we can't."

We made doubly sure.

We made very doubly sure. We knocked ourselves out, and we had a wonderful time.

And afterward she said: "That was wonderful, Harvey."

"Which?"

"Both. This what every woman should have. This is just what a wedding night ought to be."

Which put me in mind of my own wedding night, which in turn was *not* all that a wedding night should be. Not by a long shot, and not by a damn sight, and not by any stretch of the imagination. I didn't *feel* like being put in mind of my wedding night with Helen, but Jodi was sleeping the sleep of the just, or the just-laid, and I was somehow not sleepy. I closed my eyes, and that didn't work either.

Now if you've been following this little narrative closely, and if you've also duly taken note of my reference to Helen Christopher, the frigid witch of the Ramapos, you may have come up with a jim-dandy question. You just may be wondering, as you sit or stand or lie there, just what in the world made me to do a stupid thing like getting married.

A good question.

It started, I suppose, after Saundra and I came to a parting of ways. Saundra, tasteful though she was in bed (and tasty though she was, and willing though she was to do tasting of her own) was too much a product of Doughboy, Nebraska and too much a case-study in belligerent bohemianism to be a lasting thing in my life.

She ran out on me, she did, ran off to Provincetown with a lunatic bearded painter who drew watercolors of ax handles and similarly startling items. They didn't even look like ax handles, either. And, while I was a bit pained at being jilted, I was also a bit thrilled at being Saundraless. Harv Boy was free again, footloose and fancy-free.

And, although I didn't know it, I was on the road to Helen.

There were other girls between Saundra and Helen. Their names and faces have faded from memory, but I know one thing about them all. Each was not so delightful as Saundra, and each was better than Helen. I can be very sure of the final part of that sentence. If *any* woman were ever *worse* than Helen, I am sure I would not forget her so easily.

I was living the fine life of a bachelor, and I was secure at MGS-R&S, having proved my dedication to the advertising profession by planting a stiletto in Faggy Fehringer's gray flannel back. I was living Riley's proverbial life, and do you know what I did?

I decided I was making a mistake.

It was the old Mad-Ave hard sell, I suppose. All my colleagues were married men, most of them with children. Most of my colleagues lived in Fairfield County or Westchester county or Rockland County, and all of that group chatted amiably about crabgrass and commuting and the club car of the old 8:02.

And I was left out.

The others were also married, only they lived in cooperative apartments in Manhattan, and they chatted amiably about bomb shelters and maintenance fees and such.

So again I was left out. I was there, snug in my Barrow Street bunghole, sleeping with every passable woman who crossed my path, and envying the married ones their security and stability and stodginess. I looked out at Barrow Street and wished I had crabgrass to mow. I looked at my current paramour and wished she would have children so that we could go to PTA meetings.

The beginning of the end—

When a man shops for a car, he determines just how much money he is going to spend, and he determines where he can get the best car for his money, and then he goes out and test drives that car. If he likes what he's driving, he buys. If not, he keeps looking.

You would think that a man would be just as careful when choosing a wife. If nothing else, there's the fact that you can't trade in your wife every two years. If you do, the expense is over-powering. Your wife is most usually a lifetime acquisition, for either your lifetime or hers, and such an acquisition should be acquired intelligently. A man should be careful, finding out first just what he wants, and then finding the girl to fill those requirements to the nth degree.

I was a poor shopper. In the first place, I selected a girl whom, I thought, I had much in common with. I based this guess on the fact that she, too, was in advertising. I ignored her personality, and I ignored her background, and in short I ignored everything other than the fact that she was a minor copywriter at Stafford & Bean, a competing firm a few doors down the Avenue. She was a copywriter, a rising star with a college diploma and a pretty face. Obviously, I would always love to look at that face across the crabgrass.

Ah, indeed.

Her name, as you may well have guessed by now, was Helen. Helen Wall, to be exact, and there was never a harder wall to climb, including Hadrian's and the Great one of China. I courted her like a goofy gallant. I took her to dinners and shows and hip cocktail lounges. I even, God save me, sent her flowers. She was asthmatic, as it turned out, and the roses I plied her with made her break out with a horrid rash. There's something symbolic there, I'd say.

Helen Wall, an insurmountable wall, and a wall I simply could not mount. I committed a cardinal error here. I bought a car without test driving it, and few men are so foolish. But at the time it was easy to delude myself. Every thin-blooded American male has been told from the cradle that he wants a virginal bride, and in weak moments some of us believe this pap. I managed to con myself into thinking thusly. Helen was virginal as the driven snow, I would say in odd moments to myself. She shall be a perfect helpmate, a wife I can truly respect. Why a square inch of traditionness tissue should make her worthy of respect is now outside my ken, but at the time it seemed flawlessly logical.

I proposed, on bended knee.

She accepted, with tears in her eyes. We were married, she in a white gown and I in a rented tuxedo, and we cruised Bermuda-ward on our honeymoon. We spent our wedding night on the ship, and quite a night it was . . .

But I digress. To Hell, for the moment, with Helen. Let us get back to Jodi, my newer bride.

We awoke the next morning, arm in arm, and we greeted the day as days should be greeted. Then, an hour or so later, we got out of our big double bed, took a big double shower together, dressed, and drove to New York. I dropped her at the hotel and told her to call Al for the cargo and the airlines office for reservations to Rio de Janeiro. Meanwhile, I hurried for my passport. It was in a safe deposit box at a Fifth Avenue bank along with such invaluable documents as my life insurance policies and a few old savings bonds. I took it back to the hotel and rushed upward in the elevator to Jodi.

She had a strange light in her eyes.

"Al was already here," she said. "He came and went, sort of."

"Great! He leave the cargo?"

"He left the cargo," Jodi said. "Harvey, I didn't know about this. I honestly didn't. If I had, maybe this wouldn't have happened."

"What are you talking about?"

She opened the door wider and stepped inside. I walked inside. "Our cargo," she said, pointing.

On the bed, smiling, was a five-year-old boy.

"I didn't know about this," Jodi was saying. "We have to take him, and I think it's too late to back out, and I'm sorry I got you into this, Harvey. I'm awfully sorry."

I looked at Jodi, and at the moppet. He was a cute kid, tow-headed and blue-eyed. The eyes were wide now.

He said: "Hello, mister."

Chapter 7

"I've never been to Brazil before," said the moppet.

"Golly," I said.

"Harvey, I'm sorry," said Jodi, of the furrowed brow.

"My name's Everett," said the urchin.

"Who asked you?" I asked him.

"Now, Harv," said Jodi. "It isn't *his* fault."

"Everett Whittington," said the talking albatross.

"Hail and farewell, Everett Whittington," I told him and, to Jodi: "Remember me to the gang."

"Harvey, please!"

My hand on the doorknob, I made the biggest mistake of my entire life. I turned about, and I looked at them. I looked into the trusting innocent saucer eyes of the five-year-old kiddie kargo, and I looked into the pleading promising deep-well eyes of Jodi, and I was lost. Lost lost losterooneyed.

I undid my fingers from around the doorknob, and I sighed an all-is-lost-anyway sigh, and I went over to the nearest chair and I sat down. "All right," I said. "All right."

"You aren't going to run out on me, Harvey, are you?"

"No, Jodi, I suppose I'm not."

"You're a funny man, mister."

"Contraband," I told him, "should be seen and not heard."

That broke him up. He thought that was the funniest thing since the Three Stooges. He slapped his little knee and whooped in his little falsetto and generally overacted all over the room.

"You know," I said into the racket, "if I'd had a child five years ago, he'd be just about your age now. And that's the strongest argument for celibacy I've ever heard of."

But I was lying. There was an even stronger argument, had he but known it. And the argument's name was Helen.

Helen. I married her, if you recall. I recall, worse luck.

Bermuda bound we were, on one of those Technicolor cruise ships, with a crew entirely composed of gigolos, and passengers from Central Casting. The Captain was a humdrum middle-aged fag, than which there is nothing sadder, and the third night out I saw Charon pass us, smirking up his sleeve.

But I wanted to tell you about the first night out, though I hardly know why. Some masochistic desire within me for public humiliation, I suppose. Herewith, therefore, the tale of my virgin bride and I upon our wedding night, heading southward through the glistening seas o'er the turning orb toward the beauteous pearl of the Atlantic, Bermuda, tourist trap of the British Commonwealth, where wealth is common and so are the British. Very common. In more ways than one.

But I digress. Perhaps I don't really *want* to tell you about my wedding night. Nevertheless, I've promised, and so I'll do it. I really will.

That day, our wedding day, had been hectic from dawn to dusk, with split-second timing being the rule throughout. The wedding had started at precisely such-and-such—attended primarily by office friends from her office and my office—and had finished at exactly thus-and-so, in order for the reception to commence *here* and end *there,* so that the two of us could whisk away to the pier and board our vessel of delight specifically at *then,* milliseconds before the gangplank was taken away and the vessel of delight drifted away from Manhattan Island, southbound for a warmer but not really much different island, seven hundred miles away.

Honeymooners, of course, made up a large part of the passenger complement aboard the ship, intermixed with intermixers of various kinds and sexes, divorcées anxious for another try, kept boys and kept girls and kept tweeners looking for somebody to keep them, single girls and boys looking for romance (which is the ladies' word for sex), and even a couple of fussy British retirees who'd apparently been playing tourist in New York and were now homeward bound to Bermuda. Greener pastures and all that, and their presence did make everybody else look a little silly. At least, I thought so. No one else seemed to notice the irony at all. But, after the first night, I must admit that I had an eye for irony.

After all the timetable rushing around of the wedding day, it was good at first to simply sit and relax awhile aboard the ship. Manhattan Island, that crowded three-dimensional Monopoly board fell away to the stern, and the rolling ocean rose up before us to the horizon. We wandered around on deck, hand in hand, watching the sun go down, looking at our fellow passengers, and generally breathing deeply and getting ourselves unjangled.

You could pick out the newlyweds with absolutely no trouble at all. The grooms all looked gently lustful, as though mentally practicing the line, "I won't hurt you, I won't hurt you, I won't hurt you." And the brides all looked apprehensively lustful, as though they didn't believe it.

I don't know for sure whether Helen and I could have been spotted as newlyweds or not. It depends, I suppose, on how much showed on my face. Nothing at all showed on hers, that much I'm sure of. At the time, I thought it was simply unusual control. I didn't realize that it was a perfectly accurate portrayal of what was on the inside. Nothing, in other words.

As to me, my feelings weren't precisely those reflected on the faces around me. I was lustful, certainly, but there was nothing gentle about my feelings at all. I didn't much care at that point whether I hurt her or not. I had been biding my time for far too long, had been respecting her maidenhood and maidenhead till a few mumbled and overpriced words had been said over us, and now I was anxious to get to it, get at it, and get with it. I wouldn't say that I was lustful; I would say I was rapacious.

At the same time, a kind of contented lethargy—you've seen that on the faces of the cows on the Carnation milk cans—had come over her. After all this waiting and all this preparation and all this buildup, at last it was mine, it was legitimately and completely and exclusively mine, and there wasn't any particular hurry in demonstrating my proprietary control. We could relax a while from the exertions of the day, we could stroll the deck, we could take our time and take it slow, knowing that soon or late what I had come here for would be mine, all mine, mine, mine, mine.

I have the feeling, then, that the expression on my face was that of a sex maniac with a low metabolic rate. I looked, I imagine, insatiable but calm. And since Helen had no expression at all on *her* lovely physiognomy, Gods knows what our combination looked like. Trilby and Svengali, maybe.

Yeah, well let me tell you something. *I* was Trilby.

At any rate, we roamed the deck anon and anon, and around us the ranks of newlyweds diminished. A gently lustful groom would all at once grab the hand of his apprehensively lustful bride, and the two would scuttle away toward their cabin, hips already awag. This couple so departed, and that couple, and that couple over there, and gradually the decks emptied of their panting cargo, leaving only the singletons—none of whom would be making out that well this first night out—and the returning Britishers, who wanted nothing more than to sit morosely on deck chairs and think about how they'd been taken in New York.

Until finally there wasn't a newlywed to be seen. Except for Svengali and me, I mean. And I at last suggested that we make the retreat complete. "What do you say?" I murmured in my true love's ear. "Shall we, ah, go below?"

"Oh, but look at the ocean," she said, turning away from me and pointing out away from the ship. "Look at it in the moonlight."

"Let's look at it through our cabin porthole," I suggested.

"I think I'm hungry," she said.

"I *know* I'm hungry," I told her. "Let's go to our cabin."

"I wonder if the dining room is open," she said. "Or do they have a snack bar or something like that?"

Maidenly modesty, I thought. Virginal apprehension. I thought it was cute, this big and lovely girl, so well-endowed for calisthenics of the kind I was envisioning, as delicate and innocent as *Her Wedding Night*. I really thought it was cute.

At the same time. I had to admit to myself that it was somewhat irritating. I had been patient. I had been patient through courtship and engagement, and I had been patient through an overlong ceremony, and I had been patient through the reception. I had been patient during the waning of the afternoon and evening aboard this ship, allowing us both plenty of time to be rested up for the labors ahead, and it seemed to me that the time had come when patience ought to step aside for action to take over.

These two attitudes, indulgence and impatience, combined within me to cancel one another out and leave only compromise. "All right," I said. I even smiled, making the best of it. "As a matter of fact, I'm kind of hungry myself. Let's see what we can get to eat, before we go down to the cabin."

"Fine, Harvey." She gave me that beautiful smile of hers, and linked her arm in mine, and off we went in search of edibles.

As it turned out, there was something like a snack bar, adjunct to the cocktail lounge. We had sandwiches, and I plied my darling with daiquiris, on the theory that alcohol makes the heart grow fonder, and warms the virgin blood. I wolfed my sandwich, and she hesitated over hers, and at last our dining and drinking were done, and back on deck we were, for more staring at the sea.

Another hour of this, promenading on the nearly deserted deck, and I was beginning to get just a wee impatient. Every blasted time I importuned my darling about coming down to our cabin for some fun and games, she played sightseeing guide some more, pointing at this and that, exclaiming over one sight or another, and generally changing the subject by the simple method of beating it over the head. This got to be a little strained after a while—face it, there's a paucity of varied sights in mid-ocean—and at last I took the bull by the horns—that isn't quite right, is it?—and said, "Listen, Helen, it's time for us to go down to the cabin. Now, I understand, you're nervous and all that, but the time has come. Believe me, I'll be understanding and I'll be gentle and I'll be sympathetic, but we just can't stall around any longer."

She raised a hand, as though to point out a particularly charming whitecap to the westward, but then she seemed to think better of it. Her hand drooped, and she turned reluctantly to gaze at me, and she nodded her lovely head "You're right, Harvey," she said. "It's got to happen sometime. We might as well get it over with."

"Of course," I said, too delighted by her acquiescence to see the snapper in that sentence. Any of the snappers.

Snapper number one: When you say you might as well get something over with, you're talking about something distasteful, that you aren't looking forward to at all, in any way shape or form.

Snapper number two: When you say you might as well get something over with, you're talking about something you have to do *once*. After that, it's over with, it's done, you don't have to do it anymore.

Snapper number three: When you say you might as well get something over with, you're talking about something *you* aren't going to enjoy and something nobody *around* you is going to enjoy.

There are more snappers in there, but those three will do for a starter. The point being that I didn't notice any of them. I just lit up like a pinball machine, and escorted my baby away from the deck and down the long narrow hall to our wee cabin.

Where Helen all of a sudden found a whole new vista of things to point at. We hadn't been to our cabin before—a steward or somebody had delivered our luggage, and we'd stayed up on deck ever since boarding the ship—and Helen just couldn't get over the place. She kept saying, "Oh, look at—" and pointing at things. She pointed at the portholes, and the Mae Wests, and the leaping-fish paintings on the walls. She pointed at the chairs, and the bureau, and the writing desk. She pointed at the carpet, and the lamps, and the doorknobs, and the light switch, and everything else she could think of.

She did not point at the bed.

I kissed her. I had to grab her and turn her around in order to do so, but I managed it, and I kissed her, and for the duration of the kiss she was still. She didn't respond at all, she was merely subservient and passive. For the duration of the kiss. And then she was off again.

I finally allowed my irritation to take command. "Now, hold it a goddamn minute, Helen," I said. "Maidenly hesitation is all very well, but let's quit fooling around. At this rate, our grandchildren will be grown up before we start their parents. Now, come on."

"We have to unpack," she said hurriedly. Our luggage was on the bed, and that was the only reason she went anywhere near that particular piece of furniture. She hurried over to the bed, and bent over, and proceeded to open a suitcase.

I goosed her. I goosed her a good one. After all that while, believe me, I had to do *something*.

She jumped a mile, and when she spun around to face me there was nothing on her face but outrage. "Harvey!" she cried. "How *dare* you! How *could* you?"

"It was easy," I said. "I extended my middle finger like this, see, and then I took aim like this, and then I—"

"Harvey, what has gotten into you?"

"Nothing compared to what's going to get into you if you'll only settle down for a goddamn minute."

"Harvey, I want our wedding night to be perfect."

"And I want it to be tonight."

"It *will* be, Harvey, don't be so impatient for Heaven's sake."

"We've been married seven hours, Helen. Other people have consummated their marriages half a dozen times by now. We really ought to take care of it at least once, you know what I mean?"

"We will, Harvey, honestly. Don't you think I know how you feel?" (Another snapper I missed at the time: How I felt, not how *we* felt. The reason being that she didn't feel anything. Then or ever.)

"If you know how I feel," I said, missing the snapper, "then come over here and let's get going."

"Darling, all I want to do is get ready for you. Unpack our luggage, so we'll have a nice room, and put on that beautiful nightgown I picked out for just this occasion, and be really ready for you."

"I'm really ready for you," I told her.

"It won't be long, Harvey," she said. "Honestly."

"When won't it be? It is now."

She looked puzzled. "What?"

"Never mind. How much longer am I supposed to wait?"

"Oh, please don't be angry, Harvey dear. Don't spoil things."

"There isn't anything to spoil, yet," I said. I was growing surly, and I knew it, but I felt that I had some justification.

"Darling," she said, "I tell you what. You go back out on deck—"

"*What?*"

"Please, now, listen to me. You go back out on deck, for half an hour. I'll get the cabin ready, and myself ready, and when you come back everything will be perfect. All right?"

"All right," I said. Anything, to be assured of a time limit on the stalling. "Half an hour it is," I said. "Let's synchronize our watches."

"Oh, don't be silly."

So I wasn't silly. I left the cabin like a good boy, and went back up on deck, and wandered around, looking at my watch every thirty seconds or so, and waited for the half hour to go by.

As I walked, my thoughts quite naturally were sexual in nature. And, since I had not yet tasted the joys of union with Helen, I had no choice but to fall back on my memories of the other women in my life, those who had preceded Helen as my bedmates. They included the tall and the short, the lean and the not-so-lean, the good-looking and the better-looking. There were the slow and passive receivers of the male, the fast and furious engulfers, and a host of variations in between. There were all kinds of girls, and I thought about them all, and I thought about the act which had bound me to each of them and which had given them all something in common, and then I thought about Helen. And I looked at my watch again, and fourteen minutes had gone by.

I thought about Helen. My activities in the past with those other human females would be of the same approximate type as my activities in the to-be-hoped-for immediate future with Helen, so I combined memory with imagination with my knowledge of Helen's appearance, and long before I ever got into Helen's bed in actuality I had done so a gross of times in my mind. We would do *thus,* and then we would do *so,* and then we would do *suchandsuch.* It was fine in imagining, but it would be far far better in reality.

That's what I thought.

At any rate, thirty minutes oozed by at last, and I streaked back to the cabin, moving like one of those cartoon characters on television; nothing but a cloud of dust and a rifle-like *twang!* And there I was at the cabin door.

At the locked cabin door.

I knocked on the door. "Helen," I called. "It's me. It's Harvey. Unlock the door."

"Not yet!" she cried, and there was a touch of desperation in her voice. "I'm not ready yet! Come back in half an hour!"

"I already have," I announced. "Your half hour is up. It's time to drop the coin in the slot, baby."

"Not yet, not yet!"

"God damn it!" I pounded on the door with both fists, shouting, "Open up this door, Helen! Enough is enough!"

Then a muttonchops Britisher and his frau came down the hall, looking at me with ill-concealed astonishment, and I ceased and desisted from battering at the door. I offered our friends in NATO a weakish grin, and they went on by in seemly haste, not looking back.

Once they were gone, I took to kicking the door, shouting Helen's name amid imprecations. Then a few other doors up and down the hall opened, and some irate sleepers told me where to head in. I bitched back at them, being mad enough by then to want to hit anybody within range, and it looked for a while as though a dandy Donnybrook would get going in that hallway, without even John Wayne or Victor McLaglen to give the thing the proper feeling.

Until a ship's officer, called for by someone or other, put in an appearance and wanted to know, in clipped British monosyllables, just what the hell was going on around here. What the devil is what he actually said, if I remember it all right.

Well, of course, everybody answered him at once for a while, and it was impossible to get his attention, much less explain the situation to him. So I took the easy way out. I ignored them all, and went back to kicking the door again. That got me the officer's attention, and when he demanded of me specifically just what the devil was going on, I replied, "*You* I'll tell. These rubbernecks here can go to hell for themselves."

"He started it all," announced a snippy-type woman, pointing at me. I made a gesture at her involving a specific adjustment of the fingers of the right hand, and she looked shocked.

"All right," said the officer, "all right now. Let's just clear the hall here. I'll take care of things. If you good people will return to your cabins now, I assure you there will be no more noise. Just move along now, please, back to your cabins, that's it."

They finally *did* all go back where they belonged, leaving the officer and I alone in the hallway. "Now, then," he said, turning back to me. "Just what seems to be the ruckus here?"

"My wife and I," I told him, "just got married today, just before we boarded this ship. And now she's locked herself in our cabin, and she won't let me in. I mean, uh, she won't let me in the cabin. That, either. She won't let me, in other words. Anything."

"I see," he said. I suddenly had the impression that this sort of thing had happened on this particular ship more than once in

the past. He covered his amusement well, considering, and act-
ed promptly and properly, as though there were a tried and true
Standard Operating Procedure for this sort of situation. I could
see it; Manual on Procedure when Faced with a Groom whose
Bride has just Locked him out of their Connubial Cabin.

The procedure was a simple one, all in all. He reached into his
pocket, pulled out a ring of keys, selected the one he wanted, and
unlocked the cabin door. "If you want," he said sotto voce, "I can
have a bottle of something or other sent along to you."

"Thank you anyway," I said, rather grimly. "We won't be need-
ing anything at all. Not for quite a *while*."

"Righto, sir," he said. "Oh, and by the by. This *does* happen,
you know. Try not to be too angry with the lady. They get skit-
tish."

"So do I," I said. "Thank you, and good night."

But it wasn't good night to the good officer just yet. A moment later I had to chase down the hall after him and bring him
back to unlock the bathroom door. Helen just wouldn't give up.

When he left this time, I marched into the bathroom and
confronted my reluctant bride. She stood cowering in a corner,
fully dressed. I had already noted the fact that the luggage, still
unpacked, had not been moved from the bed. Just what the hell
had she been *doing* down here for the last half hour? Not that it
mattered. She'd be doing something else for the next half hour.

My bride's first words to her returning husband were, "Don't
you touch me! Don't you dare touch me!"

"I'm going to do a hell of a lot more than touch you, baby," I
told her grimly. And then I told her some more. Graphically, in
specific Anglo-Saxon detail, I told her exactly what I intended to

do to her, what I expected her to do to me, and what we would be doing together.

She covered her ears. She squeezed her eyes shut. She cringed into the corner. She did her damnedest to squeeze through the wall and escape.

But there wasn't any escape. I ripped her clothing off, not because I wanted to rip her clothing off but because I didn't have any choice. She was doing her damnedest to keep her clothing on.

I've always wanted to punch Helen's mother in the nose. Unfortunately, the old witch is dead, and I don't have the energy to dig her up just to punch her posthumously. At any rate, she was one of those mothers who spends her entire life figuratively sewing her daughter up. *Sex,* in Helen's household, was the second syllable of a two-syllable English name. That's all it was. Things of the body were revolting, all and every. Family members had to apologize to one another whenever they sneezed, had to leave the room to blow their noses, had to be sure no one was looking before they scratched. Banishment was the only punishment possible for someone who broke wind. They all made believe that they didn't excrete, and Helen still had a sneaking suspicion that the stork bit was the actual truth about her birth after all.

This shapely sack of horrors was then presented to me as marriageable, and I fell for it. I married it. And all of a sudden Helen realized that she had gotten herself into the worst horror of all. I didn't merely intend to *sneeze* in front of her, oh, no. I had this plan to *violate* her. You've heard the word. Violate. Yecch.

Violate the witch I did, too. In the bathtub. She hopped into it, and wouldn't get out of it, so by God I hopped in after her.

Once in the tub, I grabbed her nearest knee and yanked. She flipped from a sitting position in the corner to a prone position on her back, her legs all balled up against me.

I readjusted them, and she tried to get them together again. So I reached over and smacked her open-handed across the face, and then she stopped kicking and just stared at me, unmoving.

I held her knees apart, and all at once she started fighting like a wildcat. She scratched and bit and punched and butted, she writhed around trying to keep me from finding my objective, and she generally gave me a bad time.

I gave her a worse one. Making a girl in a bathtub isn't all that easy anyway, even if she's willing. If she's opposed, it's next to impossible. And if she's a virgin and therefore more than normally difficult to get at, it becomes totally impossible.

So I did the impossible.

I kept my weight on her, hampering her defenses, and every time she punched me I punched her twice, every time she bit me I bit her harder, and all the while I slammed a battering ram at the closed and bolted gate of the city. I hit the city walls as often as I hit the gate, but I had determination, and when a man has enough determination there are times when he can do the impossible after all, like the poem says.

The city fell.

And it was a ghost town.

Once Helen realized the battle was all over, the city had fallen, she suddenly quit. Completely. She just up and stopped. She lay there like a board. That beautiful body, so cleverly muscled to afford the finest in nocturnal pleasure, just lay there beneath me like a corpse. She might just as well have been alone, for all the effect I had on her.

And when it was all over, she refused to talk to me. She wouldn't even acknowledge my existence for the next two days. And we were at Bermuda before we ever tried it again.

I've got to say this much for Helen, the second time she actually did try. The whole thing revolted her, but she put on the stiff upper lip and did her best not to show it.

And that selfsame night I became an adulterer for the first time, with a young lady named Linda Holmes, a bikini-clad beach girl with all the right equipment and all the right attitudes, whose mother had apparently minded her own business, which is as unusual as it is delightful.

So that, in essence, was my wedding night. My *first* wedding night. Is it any wonder I leaped at the opportunity to have another chance at a wedding night? No, it isn't any wonder at all.

Of course, you win a little and you lose a little. Helen had not culminated our wedding night with the presentation of a five-year-old boy. I mean, there's always that consolation.

On the other hand, Jodi did. Looking apologetic and worried, but nevertheless fatalistic, she presented me with a five-year-old boy, name of Everett Whittington, and she asked me quite seriously to smuggle him out of the country and down to South America and into Brazil.

Having traded banter with the moppet for a few minutes, I sat down in Jodi's living room for some heavy thinking and some heavy smoking. Jodi sat across from me, still looking worried, but also looking hopeful now, and the tad scampered around like an innocent five-year-old.

The wretch.

At last, I said, "Tell me straight, Jodi. Is this a kidnapping?"

She shook her head. "No, it isn't. Al promised me it wasn't. It isn't anything like that at all."

"I mean, kidnapping is bad enough if you just take the kid across a *state* line. If you take him across national boundaries, God knows what they're liable to do to you."

"It isn't anything like that," she said.

"Then what is it?"

She took a deep breath. "I'll tell you as much as Al told me," she said.

CHAPTER 8

After she told me, we did the only thing possible under the circumstances. We put young Everett in the bathroom, ostensibly to splash splendidly in the tub, and we locked the door on him by wedging the top of a chair under the knob. An old college trick, that, and whoever maintained that a college education is less than essential in the modern world?

Then, as you might almost have guessed unaided, we played the games all newlyweds play. Not all newlyweds play such games with a brat locked in the bathroom, although said brat's imminent appearance on the scene within a matter of six or seven months is often enough the cause of their newlywed state. Be that as it may, there were we, a-tumbling and a-loving, and there in the powder room was Young Everett Whittington.

There was, of course, a bad moment. It came at a bad time, this bad moment did. At the moment of crisis, the delicious moment of crisis, came a shrill five-year-old cry from the bathroom.

"Hey," bubbled Everett, "let me out of here!"

Did we ignore him? One could sooner ignore a typhoon. But did we let him out? One would sooner liberate an evil imp from a bottle. So we pressed onward, with youthful wails in our ears, and I realized just how fortunate I was that Helen was barren. Life with Helen was all too unbearable without an offspring.

Helen, I thought, abstinence makes the heart grow fonder. But it didn't. Not really.

And then we were up and dressed, Jodi and I, and Evil Everett was liberated from his prison of plumbing, and it was rushing time. So rush we did. We rushed to the West Side Terminal, and we missed the last bus to Newark that would get us to our plane on time, and we leaped into a cab and pressed an outrageous twenty dollars upon the sardonic little man behind the wheel, and we sped to Newark, checked our overweight luggage, boarded a gleaming jet, and spent at least ten minutes convincing our moppet that he ought to fasten his seat belt.

"Listen," I told him, "you don't fasten that belt and you'll bump your head on the seat in front of you."

This did not impress him.

"Listen," Jodi told him, after I had made other dire threats, all quite ineffectual, "you don't fasten that belt and I'll wrap it around your neck until your eyes pop out of your head."

This impressed him. I assured Jodi that she had a way with wee ones, and all at once there was a tear in her eye. A small tear, a tear that looked out of place, a tear that looked infinitely sad.

"I can never have children," Jodi said.

I remembered what she had told me on that first afternoon of our reunion—a batch of abortions, the last one a final one because more than a fetus had been removed. A whore shedding tears for her unborn children.

"I'm sorry, Jodi," I said. And she squeezed my hand.

The plane taxied down the runway (imagine a taxi planing down a runway, if you will) and suddenly we were in the air, going like a bat from hell. The FASTEN BELTS sign went out, and we loosened our own belts. Everett could not read. His belt remained fastened. Why mobilize an enemy? Why unchain the forces of destruction? The NO SMOKING sign went out, too, and I lit two cigarettes and put one between Jodi's red lips.

She took a long drag and filled the plane with smoke. "Sometimes," she said, "I wonder about them." I asked her about whom, and the tear appeared again. I leaned across to wipe it from her eye with a fingertip, but as soon as I did this another tear took its place.

"The dead ones," she said. "The ones they cut out of me. The poor little kids never had a chance, Harvey. I asked the doctor one time whether it was a boy or a girl. He said it was too early to tell, so I don't know. Those kids never had a chance to be born."

I suggested that they might have been better off that way— that, as far as it went, everyone might have been better off unborn. But Jodi shook her head sadly.

"You have to have a chance," she said. "You have to live. Then, when you make a mess out of it all, you know at least that you had that first chance somewhere along the way."

It was a fairly profound speech, and I for once had no answer to it. I started to say that we were getting into deep water for a honeymoon trip. I didn't say this, though.

"I shouldn't go on this way," she said, reading my mind. "It's just depressing, Harvey. And you can't be too interested."

I told her, not altogether untruthfully, that I was interested in anything she had to say.

"But you've never had an abortion," she said. "It's not exactly up your alley."

It wasn't? True, I had never had an abortion. But I had been involved in one, had even paid for one. All of which happened after I was married, but not long after. And the abortee—is that the word? It might as well be—was not my wife, but Linda Holmes.

Remember the wedding, and the wedding night?

All on the good ship Lollypop bound Bermuda-ward? You must remember. I remember. As though it were yesterday, or perhaps the day before.

Every night has a morning after, and the manufacturers of Bromo-Seltzer remain ever grateful for this fact. Even wedding nights have mornings after, and mine was no exception. The exceptional element lay in the fact that upon that evil morning after I awoke in bed, not with my good wife Helen, but with another girl entirely.

Her name was Linda Holmes, of course. She had red hair and green eyes and breasts like someone in Swedish movies. Anita Ekberg, for example. Not Ingmar Bergman.

I rolled over that fine morning and almost called her *Helen*. But she had awakened before me, and when my eyes opened she came into my arms as soft and fresh and sweet and willing as— well, quite soft and fresh and sweet and willing, metaphor be damned. And I knew full well that this was not Helen. Not at all.

"Let's play a game," she whispered, her little pink tongue darting into my ear to blur the words—and to blur my vision, as well, and to make my knees knock together. "Mister Bridegroom, let's play a game."

We had played games a-plenty the night before. Did I tell you that Linda's mother had a laissez-faire attitude toward sex? I must have, and she did. Linda had somehow escaped the puritanical upbringing of my fair Helen. Salemites might have burned her as a witch, had she not charmed them first.

"What kind of a game?"

"An Oriental game," she said. "You'll be a jaded sheik in an Oriental pleasure dome in Asia Minor, or something like that."

"In Xanadu," I suggested. "That's the best place to decree stately pleasure domes."

"In Xanadu," she echoed. "And do you know what I'll be?"

"A slave girl."

She shook her head.

"A harem favorite," I suggested.

"No. Remember, you're a jaded old sheik. The harem favorites don't jolt you anymore."

"A tender virgin," I said, wincing slightly because after Helen the whole idea of virginity was somehow nauseating. "A tender virgin at the sheik's mercy."

"Too jaded," she insisted stubbornly. "You eat virgins for breakfast."

The idea was not entirely without appeal, I must admit. I put a hand on one of those fair Swedish peaks, and I felt a nipple go stiff, and I squeezed. A hand came for me—a soft little hand attached to a strong little arm attached to Linda Holmes—and the hand found the object of its search, and the hand held and stroked.

"Linda," I said.

"Not Linda," she said. "You're old and jaded, Pukka Sahib. Countless nights of dissipation have ruined your appetite for normal lust. And now, oh Great Leader, you are hard to arouse."

I put my hand on her hand, raising my eyebrows as I did so. "Linda," I said, "believe the evidence of your senses. Hard to arouse, no."

She giggled. Her hand did things, and my hand did things and for a moment passion caught hold of us. But suddenly she stiffened, pulled away playfully, and regarded my hungry eyes with mirthful ones.

"Women no longer excite you," she said. "Do you know what you need now?"

"Yes."

"What?"

I told her in four letters and she shook her head solemnly. "You need a young boy," she said.

"Huh?"

"A young boy. You see—"

"You," I said, "have the wrong number."

She sighed. "It's a game, silly. Listen, you're the sheik, or the harem leader, or whatever the hell it is. Get it? I think we've got our geography all balled up, and so on, but you're the Lord High Everything Else of Xanadu, see, and I'm the young boy assigned to bring you pleasure. Now, you have to make love to me as though I were a boy."

I told her that if she were a boy I was the Lord High Whatzit of Xanadu.

"Exactly," she said.

But once we caught the spirit of the thing it was fine. I stroked her not-at-all boyish body, disobeying her injunctions to leave her breasts alone. "You're a boy," I insisted, pinching pink nipples and cupping globes of soft firmness. "I'm just rubbing your flat chest. Use your imagination, for God's sake."

Finally she was kneeling before me on the bed. I looked at the back of her head, her flaming red hair. I ran my hands over her back, feeling skin that was wondrously soft. I cupped her buttocks, and no buttocks in the world were as butty as they. Round and pink, firm and delicious—I have never felt particularly cannibalistic, but if I ever were to begin a diet of human flesh, I think I should like to start with buttocks like hers. Roasted Buttocks of Succulent Girl—one could do worse.

She writhed and moaned while I caressed her bouncy behind, wiggled and squirmed and told me what a great Lord High Whatever I was. And then I came between them like a family feud between Romeo and Juliet, and my hands went around her to grip her breasts while I surged again and again into her.

You may understand, I suspect, how surprised I was to discover, two months later, that she was pregnant.

She called me in New York. I was back at the agency, swinging away madly in a mad effort to keep my wife from driving me to suicide. The phone rang one fine day, it did, and there, by God, was Linda Holmes.

"Harvey," she said, clear as a bell, "this is Linda Holmes. Remember?"

I remembered—some things are not so easily forgotten, and Linda was one of the unforgettables. I smiled at her memory, and thought to myself that it would be very fine indeed to see her again, and wondered what sort of games we would play this time. I decided to leave the choice up to her.

"Harvey," she said, clear as an open window, "I am going to have a baby."

Now remember please what we had done, she and I. Remember that I had entered, as it were, by the back door, the servant's entrance. Remember this.

I said, "That's impossible."

"Harvey," she said, clear as a Windex commercial, "I am pregnant."

"Not pregnant. Constipated, maybe, but not pregnant. Listen, don't you remember—"

She remembered, of course. But she also remembered that the Jaded Sheik was not my only role, although it remained most memorable. Lovable Linda was pregnant. Layable Linda was going to have a baby. Lousy Linda was making a father out of me.

"I'd marry you," I said. "But I already did that."

"I don't want to get married, Harvey."

"What do you want?"

"First I want to go to bed with you," she said, clear as a bell, as clear no doubt to the switchboard girl as to me. "Because I miss you, I mean. But what I really want is to have an abortion."

I got her phone number and her address, and then I left the office early and found a run-down bar on Sixth Avenue. There are times when liquor is a tongue-loosener, and I could ill afford a loose tongue in the presence of mine enemies, and all the hucksters I might encounter in Ulcer Gulch drinkeries were to be counted amongst mine enemies. So I chose a bar where the draft beer was fifteen cents and the bar rye was varnish, and I drank boilermakers that could not have tasted worse without killing me.

There I thought about Linda.

And drank.

In the morning, I woke in an alleyway, cleaned up a bit in a convenient men's room, bought a new set of clothes with my Diners' Club card, rented a hotel room with my Diners' Club card, ate a meal with my Diners' Club card, and quite systematically made phone calls until I located an abortionist. I made another phone call to Linda, cabbed to her apartment, and spent two hours in bed with her to prime her for the ordeal ahead. On the way to the greedy little rabbit-snatcher I stopped at my bank and cashed a check for a thousand dollars. The abortionist, God love him, did not honor Diners' Club cards.

I had the unhappy thought, while I waited for Linda to come out of it all, that she might die under the knife. This would have been properly dramatic, but it did not happen that way. She recovered, and I kissed her, and never saw her again. Yet the experience, as I thought of it now, was jarring.

I had conceived a child, sure enough. Had gotten a woman to conceive one, at any rate. The entire arrangement was incomprehensible. The notion that a few idle moments—well, not so idle, but hardly serious ones—a few moments, call them what you will, of sack time with Linda Holmes had resulted in this entity, this child. And now this child like Macduff was untimely ripped from its mother's womb, and was gone, flushed down the toilet of a friendly abortionist who didn't honor my Diners' Club card.

So I think I knew how Jodi felt, God bless her.

•   •   •

It was evening when the plane landed in Rio. It was winter, of course, but a winter in Brazil is not like a winter in New York. If we had been farther south, there would have been snow around and all that. As it was, it was more like a New York spring. Cool, clear, a little muggy but not uncomfortable.

The combined officialdom of Rio de Janeiro passed us through Customs with no difficulty at all. Our passports, proclaiming us to be Mr. and Mrs. Harvey Christopher, were in good order. Our wee one, who behaved lamblike by calling us Mom and Dad in front of the baleful eye of a Portuguese-speaking flunkey, was received with smiles from every corner. He belonged to us, obviously, and they gave him no more trouble than they gave the rest of our luggage. We found a taxi, loaded ourselves and our suitcases and our moppet into the back seat, and gave the driver our destination a hotel named El Punto Finale.

"I think he's cheating us," I whispered to Jodi. "We've passed this corner before." This after a long and round-about ride.

"But there's no meter in the cab," she said.

There wasn't. By the time I had an explanation figured out, we were somehow in front of the hotel, and the driver was asking in English only slightly better than my Portuguese (and I speak *no* Portuguese) for a dollar, sir. Obviously, he hadn't conned us. Obviously, everything was fine. I gave him two dollars because I had misjudged him and he grabbed up our suitcases, beaming crazily, and toted them into the lobby.

The clerk had our reservations, made for us via redoubtable Al. We had a penthouse suite with a view of most of Rio—a room for us, a room for the kid, a room to sit around in, a room with a bar in it, and a pair of bathrooms. There was a thick carpet all over, and the bellhop told us in flawless English that he could get us anything we wanted.

I told him a bottle of Scotch would be nice. He asked us what brand, and I mentioned Vat 69.

He went away. He came back with ice, Vat 69, soda, and ginger ale. I made him take away the soda and the ginger ale—only in Brazil would anyone conceive of mixing Scotch with ginger ale. I poured drinks for Jodi and myself, glowered at Everett until he ran off to his own room, and drank.

"He could have gotten us anything," I told Jodi. "Maybe I should have asked for something tougher."

"Like what?"

"I should have told him to send up a girl," I said.

"But you've got a girl."

"Two would be twice as much fun."

Jodi licked her lower lip pensively. "I knew a man who thought that way," she said. "That two would be twice as much fun."

"Who?"

"I don't remember his name," she said. "I knew him professionally, Harvey."

"A client?"

"A client. It was a call job, Harvey. I was working through this agency, like any agent except their cut was more than ten percent. Closer to half, really. I got a call to go over to a co-op apartment in the east Sixties. Money—you know?"

"I know."

"So I went over there. There was this guy, maybe forty-five, and there was this girl, maybe thirty. I was maybe twenty-five myself at the time. A few years ago."

She smiled. I poured more Vat 69 in her and more Vat 69 in my glass, and we touched glasses together. It's an old custom you can get neatly fried. A colleague of mine once theorized that it was the clinking that stoned you. That if you did the same thing with glasses of skim milk you would have the same hangover in the morning. A theory, for better or for worse.

"She was a sort of sloe-eyed thing," Jodi was saying over the brim of her glass. "And I thought it was a mistake, that they had sent us both there or something because some bonehead got his wires crossed. Or his fingers, or his signals. I can never keep my clichés straight."

I told her to go on.

"But it wasn't a mistake," she said hazily. "It was for real. This forty-five type had a taste for orgies, I guess. He thought two would be twice as much fun you see."

I say, "What did he want you to do? I mean, two could be trouble. Unless the guy had managed to grow a second—"

"No." she said firmly. "He only had one of those, and it was a pretty ordinary one anyway. You know what he wanted us to do, Harvey? Do you have any idea?"

"Well, don't keep me in suspense."

She waited while I refilled the glasses. Then she said, "He had us take off all our clothes. Both of us."

"That sounds like a pretty fair beginning."

"And then he had me lie down on a bed, Harvey. On my back naked."

"It figures."

"And what do you think happened next?"

I made a pretty decent guess. It was what I would have done under the circumstances, and I figured, well, what the hell.

"*He* didn't," she said. "*She* did."

"Huh?"

"She got on the bed with me," said dear Jodi, "and she started to do things. Like feel my breasts. Here, give me your hand, Harvey, and I'll show you—"

"And here, too. *You* know."

Damn right I knew.

"And so she made love to me," Jodi said. "This sloe-eyed thing made love to me, and the guy who was picking up the tab just stood there watching, and drooling a little. She did things for about half an hour and she damn well knew what she was doing."

"How was it?"

Jodi thought about it. "Not bad," she said. "Because I could close my eyes, Harvey, and pretend that it wasn't a girl but a man. And you know what she was doing to me, of course. With her hands and her mouth. I've had men do that to me—"

"Like me," I said, "for a starter."

"That's right. And I like it."

"Damn right you do."

"Don't growl," she said. "Anyway, it was just the same thing, and she was okay at it. And besides, I knew it was all an act, what she was doing. She was just a poor whore hired for the occasion, same as I was, and it wasn't as though she was a lesbian or anything. So I didn't mind it too much."

Somehow in the course of all this I had managed to get rid of two glasses and one blouse. I took off Jodi's bra. I have often been a vicarious sort, despite the rather active sex life of which I have boasted in foregoing chapters, and books and movies never fail to arouse me. A story, recounted to me by a beautiful woman, can have an even more erotic effect. Perhaps the profession is partially responsible—when you sell sex night and day, as you do on Mad Ave, you become every jot as suggestible as the rank fools who buy the products you sell.

Thus, as I stood there listening to Jodi's little narrative, my profile became somewhat annular in one particular area. And Jodi's bra went away, and her breasts were warm in my hands.

"There's more," she said.

"I know there is. It's under your skirt."

"More to the story," she said. "Don't you want to hear it, Harvey? It's kind of interesting."

"Well, make it fast."

Jodi giggled. I was still holding her breasts and they seemed to be growing in my hands. Maybe flesh expands as it grows warmer, like metal. Another story.

"So this sloe-eyed dame finished making love to me," Jodi said, "and she got up, and hot-shot took her place. And he made love to me, and then he made love to her."

"That's sort of anticlimactic," I said. "And no puns intended."

"That's not all."

"I think you're stalling, Jodi."

She giggled again, lewdly again. "I'll make it short," she said.

"You already made it long." I squeezed her breasts. "Long and drawn-out."

"The story, I mean. I got dressed, finally, and he gave me a hundred dollars, and I started to leave. And I asked Miss Sloe Eyes if she was coming. I figured we could have a drink somewhere, or talk about this nutty trick, or something."

"So did you?"

"No," she said. "She stayed with him."

"Maybe he wanted her for the night."

"He wanted her all the time, Harvey," she said. "The sloe-eyed one was his wife. His wife, for God's sake!"

It might have been a nice story for us to talk about, and to cluck tongues over, or something of the sort. But if you have read this far, you have no doubt gathered there was a strong physical attraction betwixt and between dear Jodi and I, and that we were both rather physical types. And you may have established a pattern in our relationship. And, if this is so, you know very well that we did not sit around and talk about the Rich Bastard and his Dyke Wife.

You know very well what we did.

In the morning, which was clear and dry, we had breakfast downstairs in the hotel's coffee shop. The food was good if not exotic, and the bill of fare seemed divided between American items and German food; Rio itself seemed divided between American tourists and escaped Nazis, and our waiter bore a striking resemblance to Martin Bormann. One never knows.

Jodi and I had schnitzel Holstein, veal with eggs on it, and I felt only mildly ridiculous ordering the dish in English in a Brazilian restaurant. The coffee was hot and thick and black. There's an awful lot of it in Brazil, as says the song. But very few Brazilians—just Americans and Germans.

Everett Whittington (or Everett Christopher, as his passport swore up and down) had flapjacks with maple syrup and a hearty glass of milk. He ate as though food was a new discovery and Jodi beamed at him.

"This is so nice," she said.

"The schnitzel?"

"No, silly. No, just all of us here. You and me and Ev."

"Ev?"

The moppet beamed at Jodi. And at me. He was sort of a cute little one.

"I can pretend," Jodi said. "Do you know what I'm pretending, Harvey?"

"What?"

"That we're married," she said simply. "We're a pair of married tourists, off to Brazil on a spree, and Ev is our little boy, and we are all very much in love. Isn't that a nice pretend?"

"Uh-huh."

"Isn't it, Harvey?"

"It really is," I said, meaning it. "But couldn't we call the little tyke something besides Ev? It gets to me."

"What's a tyke?" Everett asked.

We ignored the question. Jodi smiled at him and patted his hand, and I said, "Why not Rhett?"

"Rhett?"

"Sure," I said. "It's better than Ev, for God's good sake."

Jodi tested the name on her tongue, deciding that she liked it. "But it doesn't really matter," she said. "We have to turn him over to Whittington, damn it. That old bastard."

"What's a bastard?" Everett asked.

While Jodi tried to tell him what a bastard wasn't, I thought about Dixon Whittington, the old bastard. Whittington was an executive of some company or other, or had been, until he did the only truly sensible thing in his life and absconded to Brazil with seven hundred thousand dollars of company funds, partly in bearer bonds and the rest in cash. He stopped in Mexico to divorce his wife, then headed to Brazil and married a slut of some sort to make extradition impossible. His wife, scandalized, leaped out a window. Everett—Rhett, damn it—was now half an orphan, and the other half was in Brazil.

So Dixon Whittington wanted the kid—more because he was a possession than anything else. And, because people with seven hundred thousand dollars can get in contact with almost anyone, he had reached our animalistic friend Al, who swiped the kid and shipped him, via us, to his rightful owner.

The way Jodi had explained it, it wasn't kidnapping. A father couldn't kidnap his own son, not unless the courts had awarded custody to somebody else, and this they had not yet done. But because the U.S. government was rather anxious to bait Papa Whittington into returning to the States, Rhett was not allowed to make the trek to Brazil.

Thus the deception.

"It's a shame," Jodi said.

"I know."

"But I guess we have to give him back, Harvey."

I looked at Rhett. Never again could I think of him as Everett, and hardly Ev.

"Son," I said in fatherly tones, "what does your old man call you?"

"The little bastard," he said. "That's a funny word, isn't it? Why won't you tell me what it means?"

"It's a term of endearment," I told him. And to Jodi I said, "You're right, of course. It's a damn shame."

"Couldn't we wait awhile?"

"Not according to instructions."

"Today," Jodi said sadly.

"Today. This morning, in fact. Pronto. We bundle Rhett into a cab, drop him in the old bastard's arms, and scram. I think we should start now."

"Now?" she said glumly.

"Now."

"Can't we even—even have another cup of coffee?"

"Honey, we can drink every cup of coffee in this whole country," I said. "We can ruin our kidneys stalling around. But sooner or later Mr. Whittington's seven hundred grand is going to be calling for its mate—or his kid, or whatever; let's quit trying to push fancy metaphor. We have to give up sometime." I felt pretty hopeless, all of a sudden.

We were sadder than hell. We got up from the table, signed a check, left a tip. We walked to the elevator to get Rhett's suitcase. The moppet walked between us, and each of us held one of his wee little hands.

"I like you," said Rhett.

I swallowed but there was still that lump in my gullet. Ad men are horribly emotional. It's the kind of work they do, naturally.

"I like you both," said Rhett. "And I'm going to live with you forever."

I looked at Jodi. She had that tear back, in her eye, and I didn't even try to wipe it away.

CHAPTER 9

Don't talk to me about fate. It's 1946 and you're offered some IBM stock at seventy percent of market price and you turn it down and today that block is worth about five million dollars more than what you would have had to pay for it, and you try to console yourself by saying it's fate, that's the way it goes with fate, you can't fight fate.

Phaugh. It ain't fate, comrade, it's *you*. You decide not to buy that stock, *you*. Nobody twisted your arm. It's just that you're an imbecile that's all.

But don't feel bad, brother of mine, don't feel badedoo, I'm an imbecile, too. We're all imbeciles, marching along arm in arm together, with Corrigan leading the way. It isn't the fluke of fate when we make a wrong decision, podnuh, it's the fickle finger when we make a *right* one.

When was the last time you made a right decision? Yeah, you, hiding over there behind that eight ball.

What gets me mad is that we didn't even talk about it. Jodi and I, I mean. We rode up in the elevator, and we were both thinking the same thought, and we both knew that the other was thinking the same thought, and we didn't even talk about it. Arm in arm, brother, imbeciles we.

You know what I'm talking about, don't act coy. Jodi and I and the little bastard, that's what I'm talking about. A series of really monumental wrong decisions had brought me thus far to Rio de Janeiro of all places, in company with a college-educated whore and a five-year-old basketball who wanted to live with us forever. Do you realize how long forever is? More than a *year.*

And we didn't even discuss it. Never mind right decision wrong decision, I'm not talking about that. It was far too late for a right decision by then. What we had to do was choose which wrong decision to plummet into. And the *best* wrong decision we didn't even talk about.

There are shades and shades of rightness and wrongness. Now the *blackest* wrong decision we could have made, the wrongest wrong decision, was to act sensibly, in line with our previous wrong decisions, and simply turn Everett Whittington over to his dear papa and take our next plane back to New York and never see one another again. And the *whitest* wrong decision we could have made, the rightest wrong decision, was to act with total incoherence, to run off somewhere with Rhett, and the three of us remain an unlikely trio forever. Of course, there were complications of legality and income and language and a few dozen other hurdles far too high to leap so we didn't even talk about it. *That's* what makes me so mad, brother, that we didn't even talk about it. I don't mind being an imbecile, it's part of my humanity, but I hate being a coward as well.

So I bit my tongue as a punishment, and we went up in the elevator again, and Rhett looked up at me and said, loud and clear, "Whatcha gonna do with my suitcase?" And the elevator operator glanced around, wondering too.

I said, "Hush, Rhett, we're skipping out on the bill." So then the operator figured we couldn't possibly be skipping out on the bill, so he ignored us again, and I bit my tongue harder for even more of a punishment because it wasn't a bill we were skipping out on; we were skipping out on Rhett.

Outside, a gaily colored taxi was a reminder of our gaily colored homeland far to the north. I looked at it, standing there in the Southern Hemisphere sunshine, and a strange thought went gliding unasked through my mind: *I never have liked New York.*

The lemmings rush to the sea. The bright young humans rush to New York. I think now that the lemmings have the smarter idea. Drowning is so much cleaner a death.

We boarded this northern chariot and I withdrew from my pocket the slip of paper and read from it the address, and on the second try the driver comprehended, and we jolted away into traffic.

"Where are we going?" That was Rhett.

"To see your father, dear." That was Jodi.

"Are we all going to live with my father?" That was Rhett again.

"Grrrrr." That was me.

"I don't remember what my father looks like." Rhett once more.

"Oh, Harvey." Jodi again.

"Oh, *hell.*" Me.

The conversation continued in that vein, sporadically, until we turned through a blacktop turnoff between pale stone walls and along the curving drive to a low rambling white manor which lacked only the darkies' quarters out back. We emerged from the cab, and I'm certain that this time I was overcharged, and we rang the bell.

A haughty male servant allowed us ingress, and ordered us to wait upon the marble entrance hall. He went away toward the back of the house, and when he opened the distant massive door sounds of revelry poured forth, snipped off again when he closed the door once more behind him.

Guilt and indecision faded for a time from my mind, as I stood waiting for Dixon Whittington to put in his appearance. I was, like unto bird and snake, fascinated by the man. I wanted to know what he would look like. What would a corporate thief look like? What would be the physical appearance of a man who entrusted his son for a three thousand mile journey to the hirelings of mobsters? What possible face could front such a mind?

Renewed revelric reverberations signaled the re-opening of the door. I looked up and saw the face I'd been wondering about.

One thing was certain. No Dorianesque painting was locked away above stairs in this villa. The face of Dixon Whittington reflected the man. The eyes, of course, were the features one noticed first. Small and nearly round, with a darkish gray-green tinge, they were set deep in the forepart of his skull, widely separated by pasty flesh. The nose was thick and veined, with flaring deeplined wings and black gaping hair-filled nostrils. Lines of sour discontent fanned down across the flesh from his nose to the corners of his mouth. His cheeks were rounded and mottled, though meticulously shaved, and his small mouth was thick lipped, the lower lip protruding in a moneyed pout. His forehead was high and pale and gleaming, with thick black brows hung awning-like over those beetle eyes. In ridiculous contrast to the jungly under-brush of brows, his coal-black hair was plastered straight back on his bulky head in the style of Valentino.

The body on which this head sat solidly and truculently was, in a word, gross. Is that the right word? Does it get the idea across? What I'm trying to picture for you is, see, a businessman. You know what businessmen are built like, they're the ones for whom the double-breasted suit was invented. Kind of barrely. Chunky. Now, you take that businessman, and you give him a nasty mind and a life of ease and dissipation, and pretty soon that same double-breasted suit, when he puts it on, is single-breasted. And he isn't chunky anymore, he's soft and flabby. Gross, in other words. But the original businessman body is still down inside there someplace. You have the feeling that if you prodded him with a finger, it would be like prodding a thick layer of dough over a honeydew melon. Soft and flabby, with the original chunkiness down underneath. Gross. See?

I looked at this thing, this seven hundred thousand dollar mistake, this Dixon Whittington, and then I looked at Rhett. The gross mistake before us had created this tiny child, and what that proves I don't really know. I'd have to see the mother first. But of course, the mother had flung herself from a window, and was unavailable for the viewing.

Come to think of it, that fact alone made the viewing unnecessary. It didn't matter what the mother looked like. Having been betrayed by this dank troll here in front of me, she had taken the easy way out, totally ignoring her own responsibility to the child she had brought into the world.

Isn't it amazing? The most utter wretches of creation, civilization's anal excretion, the vilest black souls of Newgate, still are capable with their scabrous swords and gaping maws, in an act of loveless conquest, of producing beauty and value. Rhett, now, was surely the only even remotely possible excuse for the existence of Dixon Whittington or his cowardly spouse. How had they done it? The rose on the dung pile, and it never fails.

The troll advanced. "You got him," he said. He might have said exactly the same thing, in precisely the same tone, to a servant who had finally bagged the rat in the basement.

"Yes," I said. I looked once again from father to son, and this time I looked at Jodi. She looked ill.

The troll had closed the door behind him when coming out to this hall, and now the door opened again, drenching us with another burst of alcoholic vivacity, and a slut emerged.

Here we go again. You never know, really, what words mean. Such as gross previously, which can also mean twenty of something. Or is that a score? Or a stone? Maybe a gross is twelve twelves. A hell of a point to make, at any rate.

But about words. Take slut, for instance. By dictionary definition, Jodi was a slut, and the woman who came toward us from the revels was not a slut. By dictionary definition. But dictionaries are usually wrong. I don't know whether you've ever noticed that before, but it's true. Being a Mad Ave word purveyor for so long, it was brought home to me fairly often.

A slut, for instance, is *not* a prostitute, though the dictionary might claim so. No, a slut by *usage* is a promiscuous slattern, a sloppy slobby easy make. Jodi, though she worked the midnight trampoline for pay, was not a slut. The woman who had just joined our little group *was* a slut. Not the dictionary definition.

She looked like the kind of woman *you* would mean if you said the word slut. Okay?

So that's what she looked like in loose wrinkled clothing, barefoot. Black-haired, by the way. A good-looking woman about three or four years ago, before she decided to be a slut. Also, she was drunk.

She arrived and cast a jewel-fingered hand upon the troll's elbow. She smiled sickeningly at Rhett, her unfocused eyes damply gleaming. "And is this Everett?" she said, the way women like that say things like that to little children, trying to be cute and motherly simultaneously and missing both by a mile.

The troll—no, I'm not going to call him Dixon Whittington—pushed her hand away ungraciously. "Go on back to the party," he said.

She went down on one knee, but not too steadily, so she went down on both knees. Then she extended her arms—both draped with gold bracelets—toward Rhett and mulched, "I'm your new mama, honey. Come to mama."

Rhett, understandably, did his best to fade into the material of Jodi's skirt.

"Sober up first," said the troll to mamacita. He had the grace, surprisingly, to look embarrassed.

Me, too. Hadn't I brought Rhett here?

I suddenly remembered something that I had successfully managed to avoid conscious thought about for eight years. This was before Helen, when I was still a normally oversexed bachelor grinding away at the prevarication factory, finding my physical ease wherever I could, and a fellow pulser on advertising's bed of gold told me about Will Brockheimer's wife.

Will Brockheimer was then, and still is so far as I know, an account executive with a fantastic knack for liquor ad copy. Actually, it wasn't so fantastic as all that if you understood that by Will Brockheimer, liquor ad copy was a love letter. Will has lived on the product of the distiller's art for fifteen or twenty years by now, and I don't believe there's anything else in the world he loves half so much as booze, not even himself. And particularly not his wife.

You know how it is with booze. You drink a lot of it and then you think about sex, and you discover that the spirit is willing but the flesh is weak. There's nothing like good Scotch or rye or bourbon or blended whiskey or vodka to make you crave what you can't perform. After a while, as in Will's case, this results in even the craving fading away.

Will Brockheimer was married. Will Brockheimer was alcoholically undersexed. Will Brockheimer, so I was told, had a wife who welcomed all substitutes for her booze-limp husband. All you had to do was go along with Will one night after work. He would head immediately for the nearest bar, and drink steadily till around midnight or one in the morning. If you stayed with him, and made sure he swallowed enough to be really reeling, then of course you'd have to take him home. His wife would help you put him to bed, and then, so the scuttlebutt ran, she would help you put *her* to bed.

I heard about this interesting possibility during a particularly dry spell in my sexual life, all puns intended. And so, two days after first hearing of it, I took action. Seeing to it that I boarded the elevator with Will Brockheimer, whom I knew only casually, I started up a conversation with him on the way down to the ground, and the two of us wound up in a cozy dark joint off Madison Avenue, and Will proceeded to get smashed.

What a strange oblique seduction that was! Plying a girl with liquor in hopeful preparation of later plying her with me, that was something I understood and was familiar with. But plying a man with liquor, in hopeful preparation of later plying his wife, that was strangely twisted, and not entirely enjoyable by any stretch of the imagination.

And he wanted to talk. This man on whom I was even attaching the cuckold's horn wanted to talk to me, and I must, perforce, talk back. I must smile at him in all guile, and tell him stories, and listen to his stories, and be his pal. And all the time thrust down the quirks of conscience plucking at my mind. For isn't it drummed into us from earliest childhood that it is more important in life to get laid than anything else? Isn't copulation our chiefest goal, over mere honesty or truth or pity? Given all the choices of all the magic rings of Araby, comrade of mine, what would *your* first wish be?

And so, when at the witching hour out he passed, strode I unto the street and flagged a cab. It cost a dollar to get that worthy's worthless assistance in carting the carcass from bar to car, and then all at once I realized that I didn't know my drinking pal's address.

Are you paying attention? Not only did I cuckold this sweet and sodden creature, I even picked his pocket. Out came his wallet, and from the identification card therein I parroted the address to the surly hacky, then nicked back the dollar I'd so far paid the driver, plus another for the trip, before stuffing the wallet back into his pocket.

They lived uptown a ways on the West Side. Not too far uptown, not far enough for a police lock to be necessary or for housewives to feel frightened of tripping down to the corner grocery after dark. Just far enough uptown to be expensive without being too expensive. (I'm going around the bush this away, to be honest, because I don't properly remember exactly *what* the address was. Somewhere between Broadway and the park, between Columbus Circle and the Planetarium. Up in there.)

Will blessedly recovered somewhat by the time the cab reached his apartment building. It was at least possible, once the driver had helped me drag him out of the backseat and get him vertical on the sidewalk, for him to stand and even to walk, so long as one held onto his arm and guided him.

Entering the apartment building, the amount and intensity of qualms and queasiness I had to ignore suddenly increased, and it became effectively impossible for me to ransack Will's pockets once more, in search of keys. Instead, I found the button tagged Brockheimer and pressed it firmly.

In a moment, I heard the voice of the object of my desires, albeit electronically distorted to something similar to the croaking of a frog, and saying only: "Who is it?"

That stumped me. She didn't know my name, she didn't even know *me*. The whole project suddenly seemed absurd. I had been planning to go up to an apartment and have intercourse with a respectable married woman whom I'd never even met before. Ridiculous.

The object of my waning desires spake again, in precisely the same words: "Who is it?"

Since I couldn't answer that question, I answered another one instead: "I have your husband here, Mrs. Brockheimer."

There was a pause, and then Mrs. Brockheimer strained the building's electronics to the utmost, by forcing it to reproduce a sigh. Even through the distortion, it came through as a bitter and fatalistic sigh, a there's-no-way-out sigh. And she said, "All right. Come on up."

I wonder now what that sigh meant. Was she being fatalistic about Will, or about herself, or about me? Or all of us, equally though divergently doomed.

At any rate, she told me to come on up, and the door buzzed. I pushed, it opened, and Will plodded docilely if unsteadily to the elevator. Up seven flights we groaned, and down the hall to where she stood waiting for us.

I remember her clearly. Not because she was stunningly beautiful, for she wasn't. And not because she was startlingly ugly, for she wasn't that either. I remember her because she was so fantastically ordinary. She wore a housewife sort of dress, and old bedroom slippers, and no stockings. She had no makeup on, and her features were regular and plain to the point of invisibility. That slightly idealized housewife in the washing machine ads was this woman, without the idealization. Hair black and neither short nor long, done in a style of total anonymity. You have seen this woman a thousand times, usually in supermarkets, and you see that she was probably a striking teenager, but marriage and cookery had made her sexless. She still has the slender body and the good breasts and the clear unblemished features, but domesticity has leeched her blood, the fire is out. Or so you think. You look at her and feel none of the stirrings aroused by palpitating femininity in bikinis on the beaches. No spark shoots out from her, and so no answering spark is ignited in you, and you glance at her and that is all, you walk on.

Trepidation, I'm afraid, was the order of my day as I steered the lurching Will down the hall toward home and wife. Not only was she my drinking companion's wife, not only had she never even met me before, she was a *housewife!* Do you get it? A housewife! You don't lay housewives, for Pete's sake.

Will providentially afforded a diversion by passing out again, across his own threshold. Mrs. Brockheimer and I had to drag him into the living room. When she bent beside me to grab his arm, the loose neck of her dress fell open a bit, enough to show me the first swelling of a breast hung for the hand, strong yet yielding, full and desirable. And beneath that housewife disguise, she wore no bra!

Get thee behind me, trepidation! Housewives wear bras!

Mrs. Brockheimer, of course, had had plenty of experience of putting her husband to bed unconscious, and so she directed me in assisting her. We half-carried and half-dragged his hulk down the hall into the bedroom, rolled it onto the bed, and stripped it. I was for leaving the poor man whatever dignity can be afforded by a pair of boxer shorts, but the woman stripped him naked, and thus bare and sodden he lay before us on the bed.

She tweaked a portion of his anatomy with a contemptuous finger. "Look at that thing!" she said, her voice low with controlled anger and disgust. "What good is it? I ought to cut it off him."

"The amount he drinks," I said, "he still does need it for something."

She looked at me unsmiling. "You want some coffee?"

"Yes, please."

I followed her back to the living room, where she unexpectedly turned around and said, "Do you really want coffee?"

Perhaps brutal honesty was what this woman wanted. "No," I said. "It isn't coffee I want."

"What's your name?"

"Harvey."

"Sit down here on the sofa with me, Harvey. Tell me about yourself."

We sat down, and neither of us said a word. She leaned forward, as though listening attentively, and once again the front of her dress hung away from her body. I reached out and slipped my hand inside and cupped her left breast, feeling the tip hard against my palm, the swelling slopes soft against my fingers. She smiled, then, a smile of cynicism and animal pleasure, and quickly opened my trousers. Then her face slipped down out of my vision, and her mouth was warm.

The dress was all she wore. My hand slid up her leg, beneath the dress, to equatorial climes, and busy fingers spoke in sign language. She lay half prone now on the sofa, her head in my lap, and down the slope of my side her hips twisted and writhed. With my free hand I stroked the upper rise of hip, feeling the muscles moving beneath dress and flesh.

Then she sat up, all at once, and pushed my hands away, and harshly whispered, "Take your shoes off. Take them off." And leaped up to pull the dress over her head, wriggling her body energetically as she did so.

The housewife, with the dress, was gone. Beneath was a panther, a leopard, a cheetah. A female animal demanding the male. A musk rose from her, the scent of carnal battle. As I stood up to strip away my trousers and shorts, leaving shirt and T-shirt on—having removed my tie already and tucked it in my jacket pocket several bars ago—she dove back onto the sofa, twisting around onto her back, knees up-thrust at outward angles, belly hot and quivering, hips alive and vibrant, demanding their fulfillment. "Come on," she whispered, harshly, urgently, straining fingers reaching up for me. "Come on, *come on.*"

I came on.

It has always been my technique to tease with small nibbles, finding this works wonders in increasing the receptivity of the female, but this woman would have none of such dandification. I lowered slowly between her shaking impatient knees, pointing at my target, and she lunged upward to grab me in her hands and yank me down atop her. The legs shot out straight, then in-curved, met above my back, and locked, squeezing me down and in and under. Her arms embraced me, her mouth was hot on mine, and it seemed that she wanted to absorb me, to assimilate me entirely to pull all of me down inside her skin and make us one body.

A driving female like that destroys her own purpose, of course. Hardly had we begun when I for one was done. But that mattered not to her at all. She pulsated on, thrusting and squeezing and clamping me tight, and lo and behold I was begun again.

And a teeny tiny voice from far away across the room said, "Mommy."

I was off her like a shot, staring madly around in all directions, and seeing a teeny tiny girl-child, no more than three or four, garbed in cotton pajamas with feet, rubbing her little eyes in the doorway to the bedroom.

The woman disentangled herself from me, and hurried across the room, her flanks gleaming in the dim light of the room, her half-crouch as she ran, breasts hanging, feral and magnificent. I heard the girl-child murmur sleepily, "What are you doing, Mommy?" and then the mother had removed her, and I was alone in the room.

When she came back, to tell me that the child had been put back to bed and was now definitely asleep for the night, I was smoking a cigarette and seriously studying my trousers. Though my second beginning had not yet had its finis, I too seemed to be definitely asleep for the night.

She would have none of it. She snatched the cigarette from my hand and stubbed it angrily in a tray, then knelt before me, cajoling, threatening, stroking, pleading, kissing, urging, mouthing her need, until I found myself—despite myself—coming awake again. And we finished what we had begun. I got no enjoyment from that, but we finished anyway. Because *she* wanted to, and what she wanted in that line of things she surely got.

Though she assured me I would always be welcome, I never returned to Mrs. Brockheimer. Nor did I ever manage to feel comfortable around Will Brockheimer after that. It was guilt, of course, at least partially. Guilt and embarrassment at what I had done to Will. But it was also embarrassed humiliation at what Will's wife—you know, I never learned her name?—had done to me, emasculating me, unmanning me in the very act of proving my manhood.

And the child. I hadn't known they had a child. And I had come in stealth by night to copulate upon the child's mother, and she the child had seen me and wondered what her Mommy was doing. There was a guilt and an embarrassment in that that transcended all else.

And now I felt much the same sort of feeling toward little Rhett. I looked upon the physical father to whom I was delivering this child, and the slut who would mother him, and I felt that guilt and shame and embarrassment again, and it was almost as though I could square things with both Rhett and the Brockheimer child at one.

There was only one course of action I could, in all dignity and self-respect, allow myself to take. And so I made my decision, and my course of action was chosen.

To begin with, just sort of as an opening gun, you might say, I stepped forward and punched the troll smack in the nose.

Chapter 10

I am not a violent man by nature. My earliest memories are memories of acute physical cowardice, and I have been known to go to great lengths to avoid a fight. And that is one of the tragedies of the modern world. All our brain-workers (for this is the term they persistently apply to us boys who make the yokels buy things they don't need) have gone physically soft. We are vicious enough, and we will twist a verbal knife as deftly as Cyrano ever wielded a blade, but the physical sends us scrambling for the exits. We have but one sword, and it is a poor thing used only upon women, and our hands are better at holding pencils than making fists.

A sad affair.

Which makes it all the more amazing. Because, while my fist was in the air and on the way to the nose of Dixon Whittington, a most unseemly thought raced through my feverish brain. *I won't hit him hard enough,* I thought sickly. *I haven't hit anyone in years, I don't know how anymore, and I was never much good at it to begin with. I watch Kirk Douglas movies and an occasional prize fight, but I haven't hit anybody and I am about to mess it up. I'll pull the punch or something. Or, oh, God, I'll miss him. I'll just flail at empty air and seem like a total fool.*

A lot of thinking while throwing a punch. But my thoughts stopped suddenly, you see, because my hand ached. And my hand ached because my fist had just collided quite magnificently with the nose of Dixon Whittington. The punch, by God, had landed. I hadn't, by George, pulled it.

Not a wee bit.

I stood there for a moment and merely watched things. I watched Dixon Whittington, the troll, with his thick veined nose more misshapen than ever. Blood streamed from those black hair-filled nostrils. The color combination at least was passable— like red leather seats in a black Jaguar. And I watched him reel backward, ever so slightly, until he was sitting on the floor and covering his revolting nose with a hairy paw.

I watched. And out of the corner of one eye I saw Jodi gaping and smiling at once, and reaching to take my arm. And out of the corner of my other eye I saw Rhett, laughing like an Indian and slapping his hands to his knees. And out of the corner of my third eye—

No, that's wrong.

"You socked him," Jodi was saying, hysterically.

"You socked him," Rhett was saying, jubilantly.

"Socked the old bastard," Jodi squealed.

"What's a bastard?" Rhett asked, undaunted.

The old bastard, speak of the devil, was getting to his feet. He pawed at the air with his hands, and that was a mistake because it let the blood come pouring through those black holes of Calcutta once again. There was blood on his fingers, too. I looked down at my hands, and there was blood on the knuckles of the hand I had hit him with.

"Now what the hell," the troll grunted. "Now what the hell."

"Old bastard," Rhett chirped. "Old bastard old bastard old bastard old bastard—"

Jodi covered his mouth with her hand, demonstrating again that she had a way with children. And the slut appeared in the doorway, looking thoroughly puzzled, and Dixon Whittington swung a heavy hand to the side of her face, demonstrating that he had a way with women. The slut went back, presumably, to her bottle. And the troll fixed two uncertain eyes upon me.

"I don't get it," he said.

I probably should have hit him again. But picture please the scene in its entirety. Picture driving a furious fist into the nose of a total stranger, and imagine him getting up bloody and bowed, and staring at you, and telling you he doesn't get it. Would you have hit him again? Would Kirk Douglas?

I didn't. I placed hands upon hips and played a waiting game, and he looked from me to Jodi to Rhett to Jodi to me. And then he looked at Jodi, and he seemed to be concentrating on her ample bust, and I'll be damned before I'll let a troll look at my unlawful wife that way. So I hit him.

I got that poor old nose again, and he sat down again, and there was more of that red stuff. He tried to hold it in with his hands and the damned blood leaked through his fingers. I thought of a few speeches from *Macbeth*. I tried to decide whether a person could have a fatal hemorrhage through his nostrils. And the troll stayed right where he was again, which was on the floor.

He looked up at me. Not at Jodi now. Not at Rhett.

At me.

"Listen," he said, "just tell me what it's all about. That's all."

•   •   •

I'd heard that question at least once before. I quite possibly had heard it on many an occasion, since a desire to know what it's all about is universal in human experience and particularly prevalent in my circle of friends, but there was one time that sprang at once to mind.

It happened at our house.

Remember the house? I've mentioned it, haven't I? The suburban hide-a-wee, the Rockland County Split-Level Colonial with wall-to-wall carpets and floor-to-ceiling walls? I'm sure I have. Our hate nest amongst the crabgrass, where Helen and I lived a life of mutual animosity in rustic splendor.

I've mentioned it, all right. But I haven't told you how we acquired it, or when. We acquired it shortly after the wedding, and we acquired it because Helen wanted it. I had wanted it myself, during those moments when visions of domestic bliss had not yet been washed away entirely by the realization that Helen was colder than a well-digger's ass in Little America. But after we left Bermuda I would have been as happy to remain in Manhattan forever.

Not so with Helen. She wanted charge accounts and heavy furniture, and she wanted a massive life insurance policy with herself as beneficiary, and above all she wanted a house.

Why, you ask, do women want houses? Why did this woman, who had no children and seemed totally uninterested in accumulating any, want a big house instead of a tidy little apartment? That house, my friend, was security. That house, holding a pair of the most secure souls who ever should have graced a psychiatrist's waiting room, was warmth and stability and everything nice, as far as my icebound bride was concerned.

You see, it's easy to run out on your wife when you live in an apartment. You pack a suitcase and you go. There's no car, because you don't own one, and there's no money tied up in the house, and you just get on a plane and don't come back. But once that breezy broad has conned you into buying a house, you're stuck with her for life. You can't put the house on your back and go away. You either leave her the house when you run or you get a divorce and divide the house down the middle. And either way she wins.

Anyway, we bought this house. We bought it during one of my relatively rare I-married-this-bitch-and-maybe-if-I-make-nice-she-won't-be-so-hard-to-live-with moods, and I would have done anything then to make her happy, so I bought a house. We went out looking for houses. We saw majestic old pre-revolutionary homes in upper Westchester with high ceilings and a view of the Hudson, and I liked them. We saw Frank-Lloyd-Wright-ish contemporaries with planes and angles, and a zip level colonial with an attached carport, and we bought it. I'll leave you to guess who liked it.

And there were we, anyway, Helen and I, in our house. Linda Holmes was a thing of the past, aborted and forgotten, and I was living the commuter's life. I put in my two hours daily on the 8:12 to New York and the 5:15 to Boondocks Station, and I mowed my crabgrass and wrote my ad copy and functioned, all things considered, as a model citizen of twentieth-century America. Suburban model, that is.

Until I discovered the next door neighbors.

Now *there's* something about Suburbia. In Manhattan I had had at least six hundred next-door neighbors, and the only one I ever knew was an old wino named McHenry who wandered into my apartment one night to borrow a cup of grog. But in Reckless Rockland you were *supposed* to love thy neighbors as thyself and simply because they had bought the house next door to you. They could be horse thieves, they could be dullards, they could be syphilitics—this did not matter. You knew them, dammit. You had to.

The Sheggittses lived next door to us. Harry Sheggitts was an engineer with a crew and a slide rule tie-clasp (does that not sum him up?) and Bonnie Sheggitts was a lithe and limber copperhead. That is, she had copper-colored hair. She wasn't a snake, exactly.

We played bridge with the Sheggittses, and if anyone knows a better way to destroy an evening, I'll have to hear about it sometime. We played ping pong with the Sheggittses, and there's a better way than bridge, now that I think upon it. The high points came when Bonnie lurched across the table after a hard rebound, giving me a good look at her own high points. But a glance of breast-flesh covered with cotton is not enough to carry an insupportable evening.

We bowled with the Sheggittses, and we picnicked with the Sheggittses, and we drank with the Sheggittses, and if there was one thing I didn't want to see after a bitchy day at MGSR&S, it was Harry Sheggitts's pink face shining at me over his slide rule tie-clasp. I was so sick of the nuances of neighborliness that I almost missed out on my share in the Great American Dream, suburban division.

Then this Friday came around. It was one of those long lazy days in early autumn, and when I awoke with somebody else's head on my shoulders I knew at once that the bully boys at the ad farm would not see me that day. I buried face in pillow and listened to bombs going off in my head, dozing like a tired Londoner during the Blitz until nineish, whereupon I called my office and told them I had a small case of impetigo complicated by tertiary syphilis and that they wouldn't see me until Monday.

"I feel hellish," I told Helen. "I think I'll stick close to home today."

"They won't deduct from your pay, will they?"

The kind and considerate helpmate with her heart in the right place. "No," I said. "They don't exactly pay me by the hour anymore. You can relax now."

I had a slow leisurely breakfast, complicated by my inability to taste anything. I sat in the backyard and let the morning go to hell, and in mid-afternoon I was still in the backyard and Helen was out buying things. It was her favorite sport, running far ahead of guess-what, and she was good at it.

And there, Dear Reader, was Bonnie Sheggitts.

There doesn't quite narrow it down, does it? There, across the fence in her own backyard, was the copper-haired Bonnie. She was alone, stretched prone upon a terry cloth-covered chaise, wearing tight shorts and no bra. Her arms almost but not quite obscured her breasts. Her body'd been gloriously tanned—funny how you fail to notice such things while playing ping pong or bridge—and her hair was magnificent against the tanned skin, and I stood up and walked to the fence separating their yard from ours. I did this for a very simple reason. I wanted a better look at her.

And, slowly, her head turned. Her eyes opened, and looked at me, and her red mouth smiled. "Well, hello," she said.

"Hello."

"Helen home?"

"No."

"But you are, huh?"

"Didn't go to the office today." Inspired conversation, no. But we and Harry and Bonnie had somehow striven to *avoid* inspired conversation. Helen talked about shopping, and Harry mouthed platitude to the eternal glory of (1) the engineering profession (2) the Republican Party and (3) God. "Stayed home," I went on, brilliantly.

"Oh," she said. "Come on over here, Harvey, and talk to me."

I thought of climbing the fence. If I had, it would have buckled or I would have torn my slacks, or something. So I walked down our driveway and across in front of their colonial ranch—a specimen quite as absurd as our colonial split—and up their driveway, and there she was, by God, on the chaise.

"Harvey," she said, "rub my back, huh?"

The Great American Dream, suburban div. Love thy neighbor as thyself, and love thy neighbor's wife even more, and rub her back and kiss her in the kitchen and, when the opportunity arises, take her to bed. I rubbed Bonnie's back, and I felt how warmly smooth her skin was. And, like a kitten, she purred.

"I'm not a tramp," she said. "You know that, don't you?"

"Of course, Bonnie."

"But you can't imagine what it's like. Being married to Harry, I mean. It's not heaven."

"I can imagine."

"Harry the engineer. I thought it would be better than typing letters and taking dictation for the rest of my life, and I guess I was wrong. He's so dull, and in bed—you can't imagine."

My hands moved, gently, to her shoulders. They massaged, and she raised herself slightly on her elbows, and my hands moved to the tops of her breasts.

"Sex is a problem in logistics to him," she said. "Or something like that. Harry has a slide rule at his legs, Harvey."

Now there was an image with possibilities. But, muse upon it all you will, Bonnie offered too many possibilities of her own for me to think such a much of Harry. My hands had located those mammaries by now, and I held firm flesh in both hands, and nipples went stiff against my palms.

"Helen doesn't understand me," I said.

"I never thought she did."

"She doesn't. Not at all."

Now lest you think I was boyishly banal with that line, I must explain something. Remember when you laid little girls in the schoolyard, and they asked you if you loved them? You didn't, of course, but you said you did. They didn't believe it, of course, but it made things easier. Before you lay an unmarried girl, you tell her that you love her. It's a lie. She knows it's a lie. You tell her anyway because it's what she wants to hear.

My wife doesn't understand me is the *I love you* of adultery, the sine qua non of seducing your neighbor's wife. It may be true—it certainly was, in my precious case, for what it's worth—but true or false it must be whispered intensely before you pin the horns on the man next door. So we went through that sequence, and then Bouncy Bonnie rolled onto her back and I covered her breasts with my chest and kissed her for all I was worth.

"I need you," I said.

"I know. And I need you."

"Where?"

"Here."

"Too open. Too many people could drift around. Not here, Bonnie."

"Where?"

"Inside," I said. "Your house."

"Can't. The maid's cleaning the place."

So Harry Sheggitts had a maid for his wife. If the game were being played properly, the maid was young and willing and Harry was laying her from time to time. Another wrinkle in the Great American Dream.

"Your house, Harvey?"

"Sure. Fine. Helen's out, she's buying a store or two, we have plenty of time."

"Oh, good. Oh, let's hurry." This because my hands were busy, and her pulse was racing, and she was ready. And so was I.

We could have run around her colonial ranch and up my driveway, but somehow that would have spoiled things. So we leaped over the fence, and I didn't even tear my trousers, and we skipped into my split-level trap, she with her breasts bouncing and I with my tongue hanging out passionately.

Inside, I grabbed her and kissed her. Her breasts dug into my chest and her arms wound round me, and I very nearly threw her down on the floor. But there was poetry in my soul. I was married to a frigid Bridget if there ever was one, and I was about to bang the wife next door in my iceberg's security nest in the boondocks, and when you do something like that you have to do it right. So I headed Bonnie up two half-flights of stairs, since split-levels never have anything you can call a real staircase, and I steered her into the master bedroom and plunged her down on the king-size extra-length bed, and I jumped her.

Adultery can be fun. Now there's a campaign slogan, sweetie—and already I can hear the brain-storming sessions, with all of us sitting around an oaken table and talking up ways to sell adultery to the American public. Give 'em something they don't need, boyos. But adultery *can* be fun. Here I was, cheating on a wife I couldn't stand, and here Bonnie was cheating on a husband I couldn't stand, and what more could I have asked for?

Well, I'll tell you. I could have asked for privacy.

We got rid of Bonnie's shorts, and we got rid of all my clothes, and we pressed flesh against flesh and sighed together.

"Harry's dull," she moaned.

"My wife doesn't understand me," I grunted passionately.

And, with those rites out of the way, it was time. She let out a luxurious sigh and spread herself out upon her back, breasts rampant and thighs couchant. And, with the facility of an accomplished suburban do-it-yourselfer, I inserted Tenon A into Mortise B and grommeted industriously.

As we toiled together, it became obvious to me that one of two possibilities was true. Either Harry Sheggitts was neglecting this delightful female shamefully, or this delightful female was a card-carrying nymphomaniac. Because Bonnie rolled and swerved and buckled like a ship on the high seas, and moans tore from her red mouth, and she was having a high old time.

Remember an aside earlier? I mentioned, at the time, that I could have asked for privacy. This was true.

Because, just as we finished, just as a final groan tore from that throat and just as I filled her with the final evidence of my love and the last proof that, by George, my wife didn't understand me, there was a third person in the room.

Helen, natch.

"I just don't understand," Helen was saying. And I thought: See, Bonnie? I *told* you she didn't understand.

"Listen," she said. "Just tell me what it's all about. That's all."

I hadn't had an answer for Helen. We survived that domestic crisis, although the Sheggittses moved to Fairfield County not long afterward, but I had no answer at the time. But now, looking down at the bloody form of the troll, I did have an answer. God knows where it came from. Madison Avenue trains one well—I'd been thinking on my feet for years, and I knew how, by George.

"Sure," I said. "I'll tell you, you rotten bastard."

I dipped into my jacket pocket, yanked my wallet free, flipped it open and gave him a very brief peek at a card. The card entitled me to charge gasoline purchases at any Esso station in the world, but I didn't let him see all that much of it.

"Harvey Burns," I snapped. "Continental Detective Agency. You're trapped, buddy boy. You're coming back to the States and you're going to be in jail for ages. You'll die there, you bastard."

"You're crazy," blubbered the troll.

"Yeah?"

"I can't be extradited. I—"

"You can be snatched," I told him. "And that's what's happening. You can be marched out of here at gunpoint."

"That's illegal."

I gave him a lopsided grin. Not like Kirk Douglas now, but more like Bogart in *The Maltese Falcon*. "So's larceny," I drawled, sort of. "And I got a hunch that nobody's going to care how illegal the snatch is, Dixon boy. Once you're back in the States, nobody's going to ask how you got there, and nobody's going to listen when you try crying to them. You're going to die in jail, you bastard."

Ever see a man die inside right before your eyes? The troll did that. His whole face went as red as his bloody nose, and then it turned white, and I thought he was going to do the heart attack bit right before our very eyes. But old Dixon was made of sterner stuff. He swallowed, and he gulped, and he drooled a little, and then his eyes grew crafty.

"Listen," he said, "we could make a deal."

"No deal."

"I've got a lot of money," he said, neatly baiting the trap he had already gotten caught in. "Do you know how much money I took from that corporation?"

"Seven hundred thou."

"That's right."

"So?"

He wet his lips with a nervous tongue. "That's a lot of money," he said.

"I know. That's why they want to toss you in the tank and throw the key away."

"A lot of money," said he, cringing. "I could . . . I could give you some of that money. You could go away, and I could stay here, and then—"

"No deal," I said. But I made it sound weak. And bit by bit I let him twist my arm until he had me right where I wanted him. No business crook in creation is ever the match of a larcenous ad man. It's our forte.

"I could give you twenty thousand dollars," he said. He was standing up now, albeit shakily, and I replied to his offer with a punch in the nose. When he got up, fresh blood flowing through those nasal passages, he offered fifty thou. Instead of hitting him I told him to double it, and he was too nervous to haggle. He sent a servant for a suitcase full of money. One hundred thousand pretty dollars. A fat round sum.

"We got to take the kid," I said. "You know—I have to say you skipped and I couldn't find you, so I can hardly leave the kid. It won't work."

"Take the little bastard," the troll said.

"You don't mind?"

"Take him and shove him," the troll said. "I need him like a hole in the head. If it weren't for that little bastard I wouldn't be shelling out a hundred thousand dollars. Bury him someplace, the little bastard."

That almost got him another punch in the nose, but he would never have understood. So we left, with Jodi toting Rhett by the hand and with me toting the suitcase by the handle. I had Rhett's suitcase, too. And we loaded ourselves and Rhett and the suitcases into a passing hack, and back we went to the hotel.

It had been a lovely morning.

"Harvey," Jodi was saying, "I think you're the cleverest and most wonderful man in the world."

I told her that, in all probability, she was quite correct. We were in the hotel room, and Rhett was making a fist and pummeling me in the stomach. I had shown him how to keep his thumb outside his fingers and how to put all his strength into his punch, but he wasn't doing much damage.

"Bastard," he said, belting me. "Bastard."

He was cuter than a bedbug.

"Harvey?"

"Mmmmm."

"What do we do now?"

"We don't go back to the States," I said.

"Good."

"Because I'm sick of Helen, and of advertising."

"I'm sick of Al," she said. "And of whoring."

"I'm sick of New York," I said. "And Rockland."

"We could stay in Brazil—"

"I think I could learn to get sick of Brazil," I said. "The troll lives here, and that alone could do it. Besides, all these old Nazis. They get to me."

"What do we do then, Harvey?"

I moved Rhett gently out of the way and gripped her by her warm shoulders. "We have passports," I said. "Passports for Harvey Christopher and Jodi Christopher and Rhett Christopher, as fine a family group as I've ever imagined. We have a suitcase filled with money, and it will take us well nigh forever to spend all of it. I'm sure we'll manage."

"You've got blood on your knuckles," Jodi said.

"True."

"My poor hero," she said. "Harvey, are you in a terrible rush to get out of Brazil?"

"Well—"

"Rhett," she cooed, "go sit in the bathroom for a while like a good little boy. Your father and I have something to do."

"Is he my father?"

"Sure," I said. "I'm your father, and this beautiful woman is your mother."

"Then who was the old bastard?"

"Just an old bastard," I said. "Now go in the bathroom like a good boy."

He went into the bathroom like a good boy, and I went into Jodi like a good man, and the world went into a tailspin, like the good little world it was.

That night we caught a plane to Buenos Aires, and we tried Argentina for size, but there were even more old Nazis around and they depressed me. So we went to Chile next, and we found a nice city in Chile, and we're there now.

"Suppose they come looking for us," Jodi asked once. "Suppose they want to take us back."

"It'll never happen."

"No?"

"No. Bigamy isn't something they extradite you for, and neither is desertion."

"How about extortion and kidnapping?"

I told her the troll would never make much fuss on either count, and this pacified her. But just to make sure we've applied for Chilean citizenship. A nice country, Chile. Peaceful and quiet.

You have to get used to the idea of snow in June and hot weather for Christmas but if the seasons are upside-down at least the rest of life is on more of an even keel than it ever was in New York.

So here we are, in Chile. We rented a cute little bungalooloo on the outskirts of town and I've been planting shrubbery around it and doing other things to make it a place to live in. Rhett's at school now and speaks Spanish like a native of modern-day Manhattan, and he's been teaching us. He scared one teacher a little, asking her how to say bastard in Spanish, but we weathered the crisis and all is well. Life is real and life is earnest, and it's a pleasant switch.

I won't tell you the name of the town, because you might be something of a troublemaker. I don't think you could make much trouble even if I did, but we Ulcer Gulch boys are a rough breed and I take no chances. It's a town, and we like it here. That's all you have to know.

I'm happy, Jodi's happy, and little Rhett is happy. A splendid little group. We watch 3½ hours of television every day, we use Breeno Toothpaste, and—regular as clockwork—our washing machine clogs up from too many suds.

You don't believe it? In *Chile?* Chile's the end of the *world,* fer Pete's sakes, right? Never even heard a' electricity, correct?

You better believe it, buddy, because if you *don't* believe it, maybe the way you live isn't so hotsy-totsereeny after all, right?

So keep your nose to the old grindstone, and run yourself up the flagpole and see who salutes you. I'd say it's been fun, but it hasn't, and it's fun now, and I'm happy.

And that is why I never did get back to the office.

But on Mad Ave we always did take long lunch hours.

My Newsletter: I get out an email newsletter at unpredictable intervals, but rarely more often than every other week. I'll be happy to add you to the distribution list. A blank email to lawbloc@gmail.com with "newsletter" in the subject line will get you on the list, and a click of the "Unsubscribe" link will get you off it, should you ultimately decide you're happier without it.

Lawrence Block has been writing award-winning mystery and suspense fiction for half a century. You can read his thoughts about crime fiction and crime writers in *The Crime of Our Lives*, where this MWA Grand Master tells it straight. His most recent novels are *The Girl With the Deep Blue Eyes*; *The Burglar Who Counted the Spoons*, featuring Bernie Rhodenbarr; *Hit Me,* featuring Keller; and *A Drop of the Hard Stuff,* featuring Matthew Scudder, played by Liam Neeson in the film *A Walk Among the Tombstones.* Several of his other books have been filmed, although not terribly well. He's well known for his books for writers, including the classic *Telling Lies for Fun & Profit,* and *The Liar's Bible.* In addition to prose works, he has written episodic television (*Tilt!*) and the Wong Kar-wai film, *My Blueberry Nights.* He is a modest and humble fellow, although you would never guess as much from this biographical note.

Email: lawbloc@gmail.com
Twitter: @LawrenceBlock
Facebook: lawrence.block
Website: lawrenceblock.com